Homes of Healing Series

#1

The Beachside Cottage

Olwyn Harris

Published by: Reading Stones Publishing
                 Helen Brown & Wendy Wood
                 Woodwendy1982.wixsite.com/readingstones
Cover Design: Wendy Wood

For more copies contact the publisher at:

Glenburnie Homestead
212 Glenburnie Road
ROB ROY NSW 2360
Mobile: 0422 577 663
Email: hbrown19561@gmail.com

For those who have shared your journey of healing with me. Your courage as you walk towards your experience of home is inspiring.

1.

Eliza-Beth reached for another box and placed it on the counter.

"Is that all Ma'am? Is this all of your usual order?"

The lady picked up her packages and spoke with a clipped tongue.

"That will have to do I suppose." The grim line of her mouth indicated that she had indeed missed something.

"If there is something else, Ma'am, I would be happy t…"

"I am too busy to go into it now. You'll get used to it soon enough."

Eliza-Beth wrote up the receipt with the distinct sense that she was failing a test. It was like the shoppers wanted to see if her memory served her well enough to get their orders right. As far as she could tell customer service was an unreasonable guessing game. How could she remember what she was never told?

Mr William Madsen looked up from the squatter's chair where he sat with his pipe in the shade by the front door, observing the comings and goings of the people of Farthing. This part of the pavement, under the awning that splashed the signage for the stock and station agency, was his community lookout.

"Morning Mrs Caversham. Did they get your chook feed from the back?"

She held herself straight. "Humph! I thought a Perkins would have more grasp. Are you sure this is the right sort of place for a girl?"

"Well you know what they say: can't have pretty and smart. So, doesn't hurt to have pretty until we can find someone with the smarts. My apologies Mrs Caversham for the inconvenience. Where's your cart – I'll get Bill to load it for you straight away. We'll just carry it over onto next week's docket for you, so we won't hold you up." He bellowed and Bill scurried to attend his father's bidding.

Eliza-Beth's face flushed red as she had heard Mr Madsen's terse accusation from his overseer's post. When Bill handed her a note with a curt explanation of what needed to be added to the next week's account, she took it with a sober frown on her forehead. "I did ask her if there was anything else. She said that was all."

"She always gets chook feed on the second week."

"But how do I remember if she doesn't remind me?"

"Well, you've been told now... so you remember it."

"There are so many customers. I don't know how I am going to get it all right."

"You just do. It's your job to know."

Tears of frustration sprinkled on her lashes. She had never felt so stupid and humiliated in all of her life. Was Mr Madsen right? Was she really so dumb? Keeping shop had none of the positives she had tried so hard to hope for. She had imagined wearing smart dresses and exchanging smiles while wrapping up parcels and being offered appreciative thanks. Eliza-Beth fled out the back and stood behind the tank stand. She took a deep breath. And another. Keep breathing. She couldn't do this! It was so hard. She placed her hand on her tiny waistline and tried to calm herself. She felt like she was suffocating. Just keep breathing. She leant over and was sick. How would she ever explain to Mother that she had been let go? Mother would be mortified at her failure when she had negotiated so intensely for her to start this position straight after her birthday. Some birthday present!

"Miss Perkins?" Bill stepped around the tank-stand.

She swiped her face, smoothed her hair and straightened her pinafore. Bill Madsen had been in the class a couple of years ahead of her at school. He was a snob: a good-looking snob who had many local girls fighting for his attention. "I'll be back in a minute. I just need some air."

"Hey? I just wanted to see if you were okay."

"Oh." She straightened up. His concern made her feel stronger. She hadn't expected that. "Yes. I'm coming back in."

"Okay… well, there's a customer waiting."

"Alright." She braced herself and returned to the counter.

Bill noticed her lips quiver slightly as she hurried away. He for one had been very pleased that his father had chosen an assistant who was pretty and petite.

Eliza-Beth reported to her mother at the end of the day. It was a bit like giving an account of her school day with one very distinct difference. School had been easy. There had always been successes she could focus on –friends, grades, projects, awards. But now she just smiled stiffly and only offered a vague report of boring purchases: collars and harnesses, sickles and scythes, and the nails that were placed on special order from the blacksmith.

"Eliza-Beth my dear, you do know this job is not at all about the merchandise? It is about getting to know the community. Every person who is somebody goes into that shop. It's a step in the right direction. Do you see what I mean?"

"Yes, Mother." She didn't see it at all. Wire, hessian bags, shovels and seed grain.

"Well, you just keep doing a great job. The Madsen's are influential people and I know that if you can get on the right side of Mr Madsen, there will be doors opened for you, my dear."

The next week was hardly any better. Only twice did she need to escape outside to calm herself. Once, so that she didn't shove Mr Braydan's order in his face wishing it was fresh horse manure. The other time was to stop herself from throwing cans at the toddler who was systematically unstacking the shelves as quickly as she tidied them.

Eliza-Beth had a treasured little painting of a French café and it captivated her with visions of cooking and hospitality. Edwina Perkins had refused to allow her daughter to apply for the job at the stagecoach siding, which, aside from the pub, was the closest thing Farthing had to a café. She was not even allowed to consider her second choice at the bakery. Just now, even the grocer with his produce of cabbages and turnips sitting on display in their baskets looked like a very appealing alternative. In a moment of frustrated honesty, Edwina pointed her finger and said, "Eliza-Beth! This tin-pot town has so little to offer. When I married your father, he was the heir to an estate in the city, and a bank-manager to boot. It is not my fault he was posted to this nowhere place! We bought this house because the residence provided by the bank was not at all suitable. It has been our cross to bear since, apparently, strong health and longevity are Perkins' traits and at this rate, we may never inherit. Perhaps soon, with his father's failing health, we will have our way out. It just requires us to do what we can... and that means connections with the people who are major names, regardless of their horrendous professions or the ghastly community we find ourselves stuck in. That is what is important. Jobs come and go. Connections stay."

"Yes, Mother." It was like the things she thought she had valued growing up were being systematically unravelled. What about being a good friend, or helping others out? Had every good deed been a point of connection rather than an act of goodwill? Why had she never seen that her mother was such an elitist? Until now she had no concept that a Perkins could out-snob the Madsens.

Bill came out the back door and nodded. "How's it going?"

Stupid question. He knew how it was going. He picked up on every omission with particular delight. She looked at him cautiously and put down the cup that she had filled from the rainwater tank. "I just needed a drink."

"I, well… I had an idea that might help. Want to see me after work so I can show you?"

"I don't know…" Eliza-Beth was reluctant. Bill had a quick smile that charmed the customers, but every interaction she had with him still echoed of the insolent bully she was familiar with at school. Except… there was that touch of humanity in his voice as he poked his head around the corner that first morning which she had never been privy to before.

"Come on Betty. Five minutes. You can decide for yourself if it's helpful or not. Just hear me out."

"Betty? You mean Eliza-Beth."

"Just five minutes… Betty."

"Well okay."

They were to meet down on the Town Common as she walked home from work. Her feet were tired, and she was still smarting under the glares of Mr Madsen's scowl, her ears echoing with his raised voice as she had failed over and over again. She didn't want to do this, and yet when she saw Bill's quick smile and his obvious delight that she was there, waiting for him, she felt herself relax.

"Hey, Betty…"

"Eliza-Beth."

"Sure. Listen I've got something for you, but just don't let Dad see – okay?"

"Why?"

"Well, he just likes things done his way."

"Humph." That was not new information.

He pulled from his coat pocket a small book. "Here's the thought: we put tabs down the sides of the pages, and you can write up everyone's standard orders and check it real quick. Like this: C – Caversham gets chook feed every second week. Braydan prefers linseed oil and owns a colt rifle. See?"

She grabbed the book with both hands. "Oh, Bill, thank you! Thank you! This will help me so much.

"Like I said. Our secret. Dad's big on our customer's feeling like important regulars. He might not be too thrilled if he found a book that reduced them to a tally entry on a ledger."

"Oh, I won't let Mr Madsen see this. I promise. See?" She tucked it deep into her pinafore pocket and covered it with her kerchief. "Nobody will ever know."

Bill smiled. His eyes crinkled at the relief that lit up her eyes. "Well, I know about it. And I'm not 'Nobody'. I'm the boss's son. That shop will be mine one day."

Suddenly she had an ally, and by his own confession: an influential one. "Well, thank you… Boss," she said coyly with a slight curtsy. Then she felt bold enough to ply for an additional dispensation of grace. "Bill?"

"Hmm?"

She raised her eyes, wide now with the prospect of hope. Perhaps she really could do this job after all. "I was wondering if you would you help me fill the book in? You know all the customers so well, and what their orders are… all the quirky things they get. Your father need never know you are helping me."

"Yeah… don't think he would approve. And not just Dad. The other guys that work out of the stock-feed shed; they can't know either."

"Completely understand," she said quickly, which of course, she didn't.

2.

With a game-plan, Eliza-Beth quickly found her feet. She met Bill most days after work, sneaking down through the old common where they would sit under the shade of spreading old trees. She'd write notes in her book industrially filling in the gaps until it became the most comprehensive portrait of the customers who visited the shop. From little dropped comments, she even added side-notes of children's names and birthdates, and wedding anniversaries. Bill lounged beside her, his eyes tracing her face and figure, listening to her laugh. "So, Betty... what do you call the thing we use for..." And he would scoff good-naturedly at her lack of general farming knowledge, which he assumed was common to all self-respecting residents of Farthing.

It was a liaison of profound gratitude. Bill had saved her job, her reputation and her life. Certainly, her mother's good graces. On the whole, the farmers would now nod and smile and give her a wink. No longer did Mrs Caversham roll her eyes in irritation but would pay her account promptly. Nor did Mr Braydan impatiently offer his condescending commentary on her work-performance but perfunctorily would bid her good day. Eliza-Beth felt confident enough to suggest some gifts for upcoming birthdays, and had a ready list of pocketknives, wicker baskets and lanterns as possible ideas for customers. These were successes on a grand scale.

One afternoon as Eliza-Beth was tidying up the counter and finishing the count of the till box at the close of the day, Bill came passed and tucked a note into her pinafore pocket. She blushed and focused hard on continuing as if nothing had transpired. She had already told him the notations in her book were now so comprehensive and double-checked, that he had successfully worked himself out of a job. But as she walked down to the common to meet him again she felt a flutter of anticipation. Was it possible? Did Bill Madsen, the handsome prince regent, feel as attracted to her as she was to him? That first morning of work, when his startling blue eyes had peeked around the tank-stand and sought her out, he had prized his way into her heart.

"Bill? Can I ask you a question?"

"Sure." He lounged comfortably against a tree-trunk, fiddling distractedly with the gold watch chain that belonged to his grandfather. His mother had given it to him for his eighteenth birthday, a sign that she considered him a man and hardly noticed that he had not yet attained his age of majority.

"Why do you call me Betty? No one else does."

He smiled good-naturedly and considered her serious brown eyes. "Eliza-Beth is so old fashioned; it sounds like those stuffy people from history books. But Betty? Betty is a modern name. You are a modern woman, and I like the sound of it better. Betty is better!"

She blushed and giggled. Modern woman? He considered her all grown up? When she was with him, she certainly did feel modern and grown up.

3.

Eliza-Beth felt the walls closing in on her. She slid out the side-door and hurried down the walkway. The estate gardens were extensive, and she took a path that led as far away from the house as possible. Anything to shut out the music; and the fake smiles; and the polite conversation. Nothing was real.

She gulped in a lungful of air and tried to settle the perpetual butterflies in her stomach. Mother said this was the last time. The last time she would be acknowledged as the daughter of Mr and Mrs Perkins. After tonight... she disappeared. She no longer existed.

Would it just be her identity that would disappear, or would she actually vanish? Was this the end after all? She had said 'no'; not just to protect her baby, but she had said 'no' because she really believed Bill would relent. Of course, he loved her. He had said so many times. Of course, he would realise their love could surmount all the challenges of their parents: that together, every dream she had dreamed, of being a wife and a mother would come true. But he turned away. He refused to acknowledge her and instead everything just spiralled into a ghastly nightmare. As she stood in the shadows, she realised she had not just said 'no' to ending her baby's life, but she had also sealed her own fate. Her life was over. They were sending her to a poorhouse, or a convent. If she were lucky, she might find a job to sweat out every workday until her baby was born. But then what? No one knew. Or cared. Worthless. Discarded.

Perhaps now would be better… to walk away now.

Gut-wrenching fear was strangling her. There was no way out. She let out a sob and leant over and was sick in the bushes. She stood up and wiped her mouth and her tears with her kerchief. But they continued to fall, unchecked by the dabbing.

Her mother's voice echoed in her head. "This night will stand forever as a memorial to what you have squandered with your wilful shame. This night will be more torture than a lashing with a razor-strap; although I am sorely tempted."

Eliza-Beth shook herself and wiped her hands on the layers of fine fabric and felt the bodice interlaced with pretty ribbons. It was a dress. Just a dress. Her mother had said with biting bitterness, "Another souvenir to what you have abandoned!" A strangling reminder that was already fitting too firmly even with overstrained corsets. Now she had to pull herself together and make a plan: a plan to survive. A plan that was different to what her mother had deemed. She wanted to survive… oh yes, she did… and yet it was very possible she may not. She may not be strong enough to do this.

She turned away in disgust from the last filtered

strains of music from the hall and ran along the path. She turned the corner of the high hedgerows and bumped into the angular frame of a tall man in a dark coat walking alone.

"Oh grief! You take up a lot of the path," she said irritably. She was startled perhaps, but not scared. Not of him. It was more the dread of no longer being alone to hide or to think. She needed to make a plan.

"I wasn't expecting... or desiring company," he said, disinterested in her pouting tone.

"Me neither."

"Well on that we agree. If I move aside... you can move on." He shuffled across to allow her to pass.

She didn't move. Her mind evaporated of any clear thought. What if he attacked her? It was dark. No one would see. That would solve a couple of problems. Most of them actually. It almost sounded like a sensible resolution to her.

He cleared his throat awkwardly. "Ah well. I will introduce myself then. Mr Jensen Harker. I am a relative of our hostess, Mrs Grissom... or at least my wife was." He stuck out his hand. She stared at it nonplussed. He barely seemed to notice her rudeness. "And you are...?"

"Betty Perkins." Betty. A modern name. This man was old. He wouldn't understand. She rolled her eyes and took his hand.

He paused as he noticed it tremble. "Oh... Miss Perkins? Edwina Perkins' daughter? Heard you were moving to town."

"Mother says it is appropriate that we are close to my grandparents now that their health is frail. We live with them." She said it almost automatically. She had escaped the dance floor to leave the small talk behind she had endured all evening.

"That will be a change for you I suppose."

Huh. He had no idea about change! She shrugged as she retracted her hand and the moon briefly shifted from behind the clouds reflecting off the tears on her face, shining like iridescent rivers trailing down her cheeks.

He looked at her curiously. "Well, Miss Perkins you are a long way from the dancing. I'll let you get back as I understand the festivities are partly in your honour given your quiet country life until now. I expect that you would be one to enjoy a New Year's party if our hostess' observations are anything to go on."

"I expect you do not have any idea about anything! I don't want to dance. I want to die!"

It was said with such vehement passion that it checked his step as he went to walk on. He stopped and resigned himself to the inconvenience. He would defer his mission to find an undisturbed space to wait out the evening without interruption.

"Well. I'm guessing such a declaration can only mean boy-trouble. What is his name?"

"Bill." And she answered even before she meant

to.

"Bill. And this Bill... is he worthy of your love?"

"No! But I have no choice. I wish..." She stopped and shuddered again.

He looked at her curiously... and held out his arm. "Come. Let's take a walk together. We both don't need to hear the music after all: it is far too frivolous for our broken hearts." His voice was deep and velvety, like a soothing balm being poured over her trembling frame. "I find the dark comforting. It seems more real than candlelight and chandeliers... and the night cicadas are certainly more calming than chamber music."

That she understood. Once she would have been horrified of the idea of walking away into the moonless shadows with a man she didn't know, but it was almost a reckless daring of fate. They walked in silence for a time. He didn't seem to mind that she didn't have words... or didn't want to converse. Suddenly she stopped.

"Broken heart? How did you know that?"

"Well, I confess it is a condition I am familiar with. You have the look of a heart that has been drawn and tortured. Am I right? Has your heart been poorly misused, Miss Perkins?"

"It has. He said he loved me. He even said he wanted to marry me. He said... everything I wanted to hear," she finally acknowledged.

"This Bill. Well, I don't like him. Even if you

have loved him."

She nearly smiled at that, and then blurted out her secret. "Tonight is the last night of my life. My mother is sending me away tomorrow... and I will never see my parents again."

He stopped still and turned towards her incredulous. "Whatever for?"

She said nothing... and lowered her eyes and her head. Shame burned her face... as he quietly tightened his hold on her arm. "Oh..."

He turned again and walked on guiding her by his arm. It was a relief to talk to someone who was not shocked by her shame. "I guess Mother is right. I suppose I do deserve it. But I couldn't do it. I couldn't wilfully kill my baby. I think that is wrong. More wrong than how the baby got there."

Jensen smiled into the dark; a sardonic twist on his lips that had not been moved for months. "You know. I think I agree with you, Miss Perkins."

"You do? Why would you agree with something like that? My mother says it is my Christian duty to consider their reputation."

"I'm sure she does."

"But it doesn't matter really. Tonight was my punishment. I endured it for as long as I could. But I just had to get away. It is always to be a reminder of what I will never have again..."

"Hmm. Is that so?"

"This dress will be the last pretty dress that I will

ever wear. Poorhouse rags from now on." She stepped back so he could see it under the moonlight that flickered in and out of cloud cover as they walked.

"Well, it is a pretty dress. I can tell it does suit you... even in this very dim light."

"But don't you think it all sounds so shallow... to be worried about fine clothes when there are so many more serious matters to be bothered about?"

"Would it worry you so much if you never had to go to another shallow dance wearing another shallow dress? It doesn't seem you are very taken with the music?"

"I don't care for that really. In Farthing, our dances were not in flash ballrooms like this... just a community hall and I did enjoy them... but..."

"But?"

"Well to be honest... I only went to see Bill... and if he had wanted to do something else I would have been just as happy. If you know what I mean."

"Perhaps I do." They walked on again, their tread crunching slowly on the gravel path. On the second circuit of the garden he stopped and turned towards her. "Miss Perkins... I find myself struggling with a difficult dilemma. I am wondering if you could help me some?"

"Sir... I think my mind is so full of my own dilemmas that I fear I have little room for another's. But you could try me if you want, although I cannot promise great clarity or sound advice."

He chuckled. And cleared his throat. "My dilemma is this: I am in need of a housekeeper. My wife died three months ago, and I have two daughters. A housekeeper would be a very suitable position... and I was thinking I would like to offer this to someone like yourself. In your situation, you would have an independent income and you wouldn't have to go to a poorhouse. You wouldn't have to disappear. I would really like you to consider this."

"Oh, Sir!"

He held up his hand in hesitation. "But the problem is... I am a widower. Perhaps you can understand that if there was a single young lady... as beautiful as yourself, who is in the family way, living in my house... it could give the impression that I was responsible for unchristian and uncharitable behaviour."

"Oh... I see." She felt hope drain away from her.

"So... no ideas?"

"No Sir. I think not. It would be an unforgivable slight on your reputation. And it would place your family in an untenable position, damaging your daughters' prospects. As generous as it is... I cannot see how you could possibly consider that this would be a feasible proposal at all."

"Oh! That is clever!"

"I'm sorry...?"

"Proposal... of course!"

"I don't understand."

"A proposal."

"Oh, Sir I didn't mean that!"

"But… what if you didn't come as my housekeeper… but as my wife? You would do the housekeeping of course… but others would only see you as my wife. Then it would be entirely reasonable that you would be in the family way."

"Oh, Sir. I don't want to marry you. You are old enough to be my father."

"Yes, Miss Perkins, I do understand." He turned and they walked on for a while, her arm still linked comfortably in his. "You are still in love with Bill."

"You know… you are right. He broke my heart! After I told him he said that he never really wanted to marry me at all. He wrote me a letter and told me to get rid of my baby. He even put money in. I don't love him! I hate him!"

"Miss Perkins I think the real dilemma just now is not about love or hate, but saving you and your baby from a sweathouse. Perhaps this… ahh 'situation' could be a viable alternative to a convent."

"The problem, Sir, is that I don't love you. I don't even know you! Nor do you love me. Don't you want to marry someone you love?"

He sort of chuckled then. "I had my love. I loved my wife more than I can ever describe. They say that sort of love is only granted once in a lifetime. But she was taken from me. I was not proposing that we fall in love with each other... only that we create a situation where we can both help each other."

"Oh, Sir, do you think I can help you?"

"I know it to be the case."

"Sir, this is generous beyond believing. I'm just not sure you are doing yourself or your daughters any favours by taking me on."

"Can you keep house? Perhaps this is more the issue. I can bring in someone to teach you."

"Of course, I can keep a house. But what about..." She swallowed awkwardly. "... if we were married... what about the bedroom? I don't think I could do that."

"Oh. Well. Okay. Let us agree that you will not have to perform the bedroom duties of a wife. Just the housekeeping ones. Does that seem agreeable?"

"Sir, would you be okay with that?"

"I am the one to make the suggestion. Like you said... I am old. I am also sad... old and sad... so it is likely that I would get by knowing my daughters' home is well kept."

"It is also your home."

"True. But my needs are small. It is my daughters that I am concerned for. Susanna is not far off fourteen and Eunice is eleven."

"I can't be a mother! I am only sixteen! I can't possibly..."

"Miss Perkins. You are going to be a mother... whether you marry me or not, regardless of your age."

"Sir, I really do think you need to consider this sensibly. What would everybody say?"

"Perhaps Miss Perkins I do not care too much what everyone else says... only what you say. If other people's opinions dictate what I do ... I could be moving towns, and dancing to shallow music for the rest of my life."

She sighed then. "Well put. You know my mother will not be pleased."

"I don't know your mother, but I sense she is already not pleased... so this will probably be just more of the same."

"It sounds like you know her fairly well actually."

"Only by reputation. But I have just met her daughter and I am completely taken with the idea that she will be my housekeeper. What do you say, Miss Perkins? Will you marry me?"

4.

They walked around the grounds arm in arm. Their casual, unhurried pace belied the anxious topic of their conversation. "So, Miss Perkins… I know you said you can keep house, but I also wonder how you are at acting? I think these people are going to need some convincing, because it is my observation that they are not terribly interested in the truth."

"What do you mean Sir?"

"I mean that if we are to be married, then it would not hurt if they believe we are truly in love. Now we know that is not the case, but people who frequent ballrooms have a hard time accepting unusual situations. If they cannot see a plausible reason they generally oppose them. Do you follow me?"

"I think so, Sir."

"So… I am going to ask you to call me Jensen."

"Jensen? Yes Sir."

"Jensen… just Jensen."

"Yes, S-Jensen… Oh, Sir. I can't! That is really weird for me."

He nodded and smiled. "You will get used to it Miss Perkins."

"Betty."

"Oh yes, I suppose I should use a less formal address too. Although I thought your name was Elizabeth."

"Eliza-Beth really. My mother calls me that, but Bill said Betty was a name for a modern woman. I like it better." Huh. Or at least Bill did.

"Well I am old fashioned and I think I will call you Elizabeth."

She grunted. Did everyone have a version on her name? "Why?"

"Because in my opinion Eliza-Beth sounds pretentious, and Betty sounds cheap. Elizabeth is a name much more fitting for a beautiful, elegant lady such as yourself. How does it sound to be Elizabeth Harker?"

"Very strange."

They had walked another full circuit of the grounds and the music again came into earshot. He placed his hand firmly over hers as it rested on his arm and they looked toward the lights spilling through the windows of the hall. "Well, it is nearly midnight. Are you ready to start the New Year with an announcement of our new-found love Miss Elizabeth?"

She giggled with embarrassment. "I will try…"

He went to step forward and he paused as the giggle changed to a whimper and he felt her frame tremble. "You are cold." He took off his dinner jacket and placed it around her shoulders. Tears fell on to the fabric, bleeding into the weave.

"No. Not really. I just need a moment…" She sniffed and wiped her face on the sleeve.

"Oh, this will never do!" His voice was deep and rough, and there was energy in his frame that was barely constrained. He abruptly turned around and guided her back into the shadows. He scarcely paused and strode out beyond the cover of the shrubbery as it started to drizzle.

Elizabeth stepped quickly to keep up with his long stride. "Sir! I am sorry. Please don't be displeased. I will wash your jacket. I promise. And the rest... I will try. I am much better now. I can do this. I can!"

He said nothing but walked determinedly across the sweeping driveway and signalled for his carriage. The coachman brought it around and jumped down to open the door. "Buchanan, take us home," he said brusquely and bundled Elizabeth inside. He stepped up, sitting opposite her, his jaw set, his gaze unmoved. Her tears now fell unheeded. She squeezed her eyes tight. She hadn't meant to disregard his kindness. It was just very hard. He didn't know her mother. Failure on failure.

He said nothing. The coach rocked and jolted. At some point, he took a folded rug from the seat beside him and covered her shoulders. And she shrank underneath it to cover her disgrace, dozing off to the rocking of the carriage exhausted.

Elizabeth stirred and rolled over. She felt the quality of the sheets under her fingers and smiled in her dozy morning sleep as she realised that this horrific nightmare was just a dream. What a relief. A dream. She stretched and rubbed her forearms... and felt her nightdress. This was strange. She cautiously felt the heavy handmade lace along the neckline... and her eyes flew open. She sat upright her eyes wide.

"Morning Miss Elizabeth."

She stared at a thickset lady sitting in the corner. Elizabeth glanced around the unfamiliar room, gasped, rolled her eyes and fell back on the pillows. Nope. Not a dream.

"Aah Miss Elizabeth, Master Jensen has gone out and he has left instructions for me. He said I was to stay in your room until you woke up. He gave you a draught last night to help you sleep, and he didn't want you waking up alone in a strange house."

Elizabeth sat up again and started breathing slowly. Just keep breathing.

"Master Jensen said he would be back for lunch and he said he would like you to dine together. The young Miss Harker's are staying with their Aunt for an extended holiday. He said he had a couple of things to organise. He said that I was to pack a trunk for you... just some things out of his wife's closet... if you didn't object. Just until we can arrange some other things more to your taste."

Elizabeth stared at her and pulled the sheet up

high. Just keep breathing.

"I guess this must seem very strange Miss. My name is Glenys but you must call me Glennie, like everyone else. I'm the cook... although I do perform a good many other duties. You might have met Buchanan last night: he drove you home. That's my Joe. You must be exhausted you poor little Mite... never seen one sleep so deep. Which reminds me, Master Jensen was very sure I was not to weary you with all my chatter, but I do know how odd it can be waking up in a strange house. Now I brought up some breakfast, but I didn't know your preferences... so I just added a couple of choices."

She placed a tray on the bed and Elizabeth lifted the lid. She stared at the slabs of bacon and eggs and thick buttered toast. She flew out of bed to the washstand and was sick in the bowl.

Glennie followed her with her eyes and went silent. She quietly withdrew and returned with some dry toast and weak tea. "This might be more to your liking Miss. Don't worry. It usually settles down some... after a bit."

"I'm here to meet with Mr Frank Perkins."

"Wait here, Sir." He stood by the mantle and patiently formulated his words. When Mr Perkins walked in he was still in his morning smoking jacket. His eyes were bloodshot, and he looked like he had slept very little. He stuttered his confusion when Jensen stepped forward and shook his hand.

"Mr Jensen Harker. I know I do not have an appointment, and you must be wondering about this strange diversion from protocol so I will get directly to the point of my visit. I wish to ask for your daughter's hand in marriage."

Mr Perkins sat down hard. "Eliza… she is okay?"

"She is unsettled and very uncertain about her future. But in this, I can help. We have agreed to marry as soon as possible."

"Oh."

Jensen looked at this man sitting there wiping his brow and tried very hard not to despise his spineless disposition or lack of any true conviction. "Sir I think it would be fair to acknowledge our minds are already determined on this course, so with or without your blessing we will proceed."

"You seem sure. You know what you are getting?"

"Yes, Sir, I do."

He stood up and shook his hand. "How much are you requiring as dowry?"

"I will not be asking for any Sir. Just your blessing."

He stared at him a little incredulously but didn't seem to want to clarify in case he changed his mind. "Then you have it. I will let my wife know.

Please excuse her. She is quite distraught because our daughter... she disappeared last night... after the ball without a trace. We supposed..." His voice trailed off and the thought was never completed.

Jensen looked at him and mildly observed. "Well, now you can reassure her mind."

"Oh yes. Of course."

"Francis, have you seen where they put my..." Mrs Perkins swept into the room dressed in black satin and stopped suddenly. "Oh, I am sorry," she paused and sniffed, "I didn't realise you had company. It is Mr Jensen Harker... the architect, is it not?"

"It is Ma'am. Pleased to make your acquaintance." He nodded.

"Mr Harker you will have to excuse us from taking any business calls this morning. We are in the middle of the most tragic family crisis. Our daughter..." She sniffled and groaned and started weeping.

Jensen was completely unmoved by their tragedy and looked from Elizabeth's father who stood there agitated and speechless, to her mother sobbing hysterically into the kerchief. "Well, Mr Perkins can relay my news, as I can see you are completely and utterly overcome with grief." He turned to go.

"Oh, we are, kind Sir. We are. If you would like to come back next week perhaps we could talk about starting some remodelling designs for our estate then. We won't be able to start the work immediately of course but I think it would be entirely reasonable to have some concept plans in place."

"I'm sorry I won't be available next week, but I can refer one of my associates to your attention. I will be away on my honeymoon Ma'am," he added.

"Honeymoon? Oh, I do like a wedding. Mrs Grissom didn't mention you were engaged. Although she did say you had lost your wife in the most tragic of circumstances, and she had insisted you attend. Was the lady here with you last night?"

"She was. Yes." He swallowed hard, gathered his hat from the sideboard, and bowed. "My condolences for your loss, Ma'am." He fully intended to leave it at that. Mr Perkins stood at the door, his mouth gaping like a fish. "I will be sure to pass news of your wellbeing on to your daughter, as I know she will be saddened by your profound grief."

The effect was entirely miraculous. "Eliza-Beth! Do you know where she is? I thought that... what I mean is... we have been out of our minds with worry. You should have said something!"

"I already did. Your husband can relay our conversation, as I have some rather important matters I need to attend to."

Edwina's eyes narrowed from under the edge of her veil. "What conversation? What have you done?"

"I have asked her to marry me."

"That tramp! Is there nothing that she would

not do to steal my peace of mind?" She paused. "And yet you would entrap yourself in a marriage you cannot escape?"

He could almost have sworn she looked at her husband... or past him, when she said that. "Duly noted. Like you, I always thought marriage was forever... and yet here I am a widower."

"What bride-price are you offering? What will you give us?"

"What makes to think I have come here to trade for your daughter like horse-flesh? It was courtesy call only... to inform you of our intended nuptials."

"Well that is very offensive, given the distress we are under just now!" She raised her black kerchief and lowered her veil... and sniffed. "A man of your means could offer something."

He almost reached for his chequebook, until he saw a glint in her eye that reminded him of a black scavenger crow. His hand went inside his jacket, and instead, he pulled out his large handkerchief and offered it to her. "Your own kerchief hardly seems adequate for the scale of your distress Ma'am."

Edwina stared at it and then hissed, "You will go away for at least a month and not breathe a word of this until you are settled back home."

"If you insist."

"I do... and if there is any hint of this coming to light before the month is out, there will be such a scandal that you will never work in this town again. Be warned, Mr Harker. I am formidable."

He bowed again. "I cannot disagree, Mrs Perkins."

Jensen strode into the library and threw his gloves and scarf over the back of the chesterfield. He went to his desk and poured himself a drink. "Glennie!" Glennie duly appeared. "Where is she? We will have lunch in here."

Glennie said nothing but directed her glance over to the shadows where a small frame emerged from the recesses of a reading chair.

"Oh. Well, leave us now. I will ring when we are ready to eat," he added as she left and closed the door behind her.

Elizabeth stood up and he jolted as he looked at her standing in a plain dark blue dress that Glennie had provided for her. It didn't fit perfectly, and it was a little too long... but was suitable for sure. At least she had thought so.

He stood in the middle of his library in his riding boots and coat, and suddenly seemed lost for words. He took off his coat and draped it over his desk chair as if he was vying for time. "I... ahh... trust you slept well... even in a strange place?"

"I did Sir... thank you."

This man had been kind as they walked the

shadows of the garden. He had broken just about every known code of etiquette, but he had done it so sympathetically that it didn't seem so bad. But then, Bill had been kind to her once upon a time too.

He smiled. "Did we not agree that you were to call me Jensen? No tripping up for appearances if we make it our standard form of address."

"Yes, Sir... Jensen."

He scoffed. "That is even more ridiculous... Sir Jensen."

"Sorry, Sir... Sorry. I did not mean to give the impression I was mocking you. It seems to be a pattern of mine... discounting the generosity of others. So, I understand completely that you would want to disregard our discussion from last night."

"Why ever would you say that? Believe me, I am not forgetting anything."

"But you left this morning... and... and..."

"I told Glennie to relay the message that I had some business to attend to. What did you think I was doing?"

"Well, Sir... Glennie did pass on your message. You are obviously regretting flouting the rules and making..."

"Obviously. Regretting what rules?"

"Well, Sir the list is very long... and I only refer to the usual ones."

"Really? Which ones disturb me exactly?" He looked at her mildly with a focused glint in his eye.

"Well, you spoke to me even though I left the dance unaccompanied. We walked the grounds together for a long time – just you and me, without a chaperone. You took me to your home in your carriage... together. I stayed here... overnight."

He tilted his head just a little. It gave his face an elongated sort of appearance. "Do you think I did these things to shame you?"

"Oh no, Sir. I thought you were very kind... until... well, you sent your daughters away so that they would avoid meeting me. So, it seems to me that you are taking my advice after all and organising to hide me away."

"Is that what you think?"

"Of course, Sir... but I do not blame you. It is just the way things are."

He huffed irritably. "Not in this house." He rang the bell impatiently. "I think we need to eat. I'm starved and you look like you are going to fall over. Perhaps hunger is spoiling your clear thinking. You seemed much more sensible last night. Sit there and we can talk while we eat. Don't panic... just something light." He poured her a glass of water and didn't clarify whether he meant the food or the conversation.

Glennie hustled in with a tray. She arranged it on the low table and fussed with the arrangement of the napkins. "Oh, just leave it. Glennie! Not now. Please."

She bowed and exited, closing the door just a little too firmly. Jensen hardly noticed. He was focused on Elizabeth's drawn face and furrowed brow. He quietly said a prayer under his breath. "God of all wisdom…"

"Would you like some fruit?" he said indicating the platter. "Apricots are in season."

She nodded and he added a selection to a side plate and handed it to her. She took it and ate slowly almost as if she had to focus hard on each bite. Suddenly she stopped. "Oh, Sir I am so sorry! This is very presumptuous of me. I should be serving you." She quickly put down her plate and jumped up.

"Oh please. Later. You can do that later. It is just us in here… so there is no need for ceremony." He nodded to her place and waved. "Sit down. I think some things need clarification."

She meekly complied and sat.

"Elizabeth. You are going to be my wife, so there are things that need attention in preparation for this."

"Sir! Surely you are not going ahead? That is not a good idea!"

"After this morning I couldn't be more certain that this is the best idea."

"But last night… you were so irritated with me. I displeased you so severely. I sniffed on your sleeve. It is probably right that I disappear."

"What? You think I am worried about my

sleeve? That's ridiculous!"

"It was a very common and unmannerly thing to do, even if I was distraught. I should not have done that."

"Huh! It is not often I let these things... these people... get on top of me. When I saw how distressed you were, I couldn't think of putting you through the scrutiny of a public engagement. That is why I brought you straight home."

"Engagement?"

"Yes Elizabeth, remember this is the plan. To get married we have to be engaged. I rode over to Grissom's Estate this morning and spoke with your father. He is agreeable to the marriage. I also spoke to your mother. She is not agreeable on anything. She is wearing black: already in mourning, because you disappeared. What a ridiculous display! Her compliance is dependent on no one knowing anything until we get back from our honeymoon. That will give her time for her theatrics I suspect. I am surprised you are not more of an actor. Your mother is very accomplished."

"Honeymoon?" She went a little pale.

He sounded a little impatient. "I do remember our bedroom agreement. But we both have to get our heads around some very big changes, and I think some time away will be a way to do this. I will not subject you to the standard wedding tour; we will go somewhere quiet. To continue to be convincing these things go hand-in-hand. So, the only disappearing you will be doing for the moment is for our honeymoon."

He poured himself a cup of tea and ate some of the chicken that was on the plate. He dipped his fingers in the fingerbowl, wiped them on a napkin and put it aside. "Tea?"

Elizabeth shook her head.

"Finished eating?"

She nodded.

"Hmm. Well, I did do something else while I was out. I went shopping."

"Really Sir? My father would never do shopping himself." Mr Harker was very unconventional.

"I wouldn't normally either, but this was something that I wanted to attend to myself."

He pulled from his pocket a small silk-covered box that shimmered in the light, trimmed with gold braid around the lid. He came around beside her and knelt by her chair. She went to jump up, but he restrained her gently by placing his hand on her arm. "Miss Elizabeth, would you do me the honour of wearing this ring that I have bought for you?

He waited for her to reply, but all that she could manage was a shudder followed by a flood of tears. He gently lifted her hand and kissed her fingers and opened the box to reveal an exquisite gold filigree band with an enormous diamond, studded with a circle of emeralds and rubies. He took the ring and slid it on her finger.

She stared at it dumbfounded. Even if she was going to be hidden away, everything was proper. She felt her shame peeling off… layer by layer. "Oh, Sir! Thank you!" She flung herself forward and wrapped her arms around his neck. "Thank you, Sir, from the bottom of my heart. Sir, I assure you I will be the very best housekeeper you have ever had. I promise Sir. I will work very hard. You will not be disappointed."

He swallowed and closed his eyes as he waited for her to sit back in her chair. Then he stood up and poured himself another cup of tea. "I was not sure what gems you are partial to, so I determined you would have as many as could be found in one setting. I could not wait to have a ring especially designed so I hope this is to your liking."

"Sir, this is beyond generous. It is very beautiful." She held her hand out in front of her, staring at the colours glinting in the sunlight through the window.

His mouth sort of smiled on one side in a melancholy way.

"Sir? When will I start the housekeeping?"

"Ahh. The duties of a wife. Well, I have some very high expectations on that front."

"Oh, I know Sir. I will not let you down."

"So… this afternoon you have to go shopping."

"Oh? Yes of course Sir. Whatever you need."

"Hmm. I need my fiancé to find a wedding

gown and some slippers. There is a nice little boutique shop close by that my wife used to adore. Perhaps you will like it too."

"You want me to go shopping... for me?"

"No – this is absolutely for me, because tomorrow we leave... to marry."

"Tomorrow?"

"Yes. It would be unseemly to delay any longer. As you rightly observed... we are staying under the same roof."

"Oh. Yes. Of course."

"So? Can you do that, or do you need me along?"

She wondered how she could say it. "Sir... I did work for a reasonable time... and the wages as a shop assistant were not much. But, it's just that mother insisted my money be held for... well, she called it my 'Wedding Fund'. But as you probably guess, I don't have access to it now. I am sorry Sir, but Glennie did show me some very fine gowns... and I could choose one of those."

He looked at her curiously. "I must apologise Miss Elizabeth I did not mean to cause you anxiety. Of course, I do understand this could be an expensive exercise."

"Oh no Sir, it is no bother. I am not worried. I just don't want you to be disappointed."

"You know, I think I will come along. I fully intend... since this is shopping for my purposes that I will be responsible for the account. This can be our first outing as betrothed."

"But Sir, you said you didn't do shopping and I thought that it was bad luck if the groom saw the gown before the wedding."

"Do you feel I bring you bad luck, Miss Elizabeth?"

"Oh no. Not at all, Sir. I just don't want to curse our wedding."

"I'm not superstitious by nature, and I always thought anticipation was ninety percent of the fun. I'm sure it will be okay since I find you a blessing."

"You do? Well, if you are sure?"

"I'm sure. Have you eaten enough? Be sure you have all the stamina you need for bridal shopping. I understand it can be quite an ordeal."

He stood as Elizabeth left to get ready. He had wanted to avoid that shop. It had been Georgina's favourite shopping haunt. He took a deep breath and whispered a prayer. "Oh Georgina, I think you would like her. She is so lost and scared. I trust some gentleman would do the same for our Susanna or Eunice if life turned against them like this. I trust you do understand. Please God in Heaven, explain it to her…"

Glennie prattled all the way to the shop about the best sort of fabrics that were easy to clean, and the cut of the neckline that was most flattering and the most practical shoes. Elizabeth hardly heard. It was very strange not to be just presented for a final fitting and told what function it was for. Even in little old Farthing, a small town with hardly any shops, Mother would take in her catalogues and have the dressmaker replicate the latest fashion, although mostly they were in more practical fabrics.

Jensen met the proprietor, a mature lady with a wide bustle, on the step as she unlocked the door. As it was New Year's Day, he had especially arranged this private sitting with the appropriate remuneration. He removed his hat and plunged inside as if entering a burning building. He was grateful no other customers would be browsing today. He paused at the counter as the assistant came in and recognised him. Jensen glanced at Elizabeth who was working her way towards a far rack of very drab dresses. He lowered his voice and adjusted his jacket so that his black sleave bands were just visible. There was a quiet exclamation of "I am so very sorry Mr Harker! Mrs Harker was such a favourite of ours." He leant over and whispered a few words requiring discretion. "I understand perfectly. Perfectly Sir." He handed the lady a generous tip, and she watched him walk away with a sigh. "Oh, my dear, dear poor Georgina."

Jensen removed his gloves and sat on the lounge provided for those attending their clientele. This shop didn't have customers; they only had patrons. He sat tall and stiff while the parade began. Elizabeth emerged wearing a very limp second-hand gown, which originally had probably been pink but was now a dull sort of peachy colour.

Jensen frowned and cleared his throat and indicated that she come closer. "Elizabeth dear? I have a couple of expectations here. It must be pretty. It must be white... and it must be today. We don't have the luxury of ordering a custom gown, so any alterations have to be done today. Nothing else matters."

Her eyes widened and she froze. She knew exactly what he was saying. The lady came and quickly guided her back to the dressing room, and apologetically offered, "I think there has been a mistake. This was on the discard rack. I am sure there are other gowns that might be more to your liking." Then she stuck her head out of the dressing room and immediately pointed an angular finger to her assistant to run to her bidding. Glennie said later with a laugh that she could hear the money clanging so loudly in their heads, that she thought the rag and bone man was doing his rounds.

The attendant very discretely walked past Mr Harker who would nod or frown according to his opinion. Every so often he would raise his brow as Elizabeth modelled the dress or indicate a look from another aspect with a twirl of his long finger; then he would consult with Glennie before offering a nod or shake his head with a frown. The Nod Pile was much smaller than the Frown Pile.

Finally, the lady regretfully noted, "This gown Mr Harker, is the last one we have on the mannequins."

"I'm sure we have something we can work with here. So, Elizabeth, which of these beauties takes your fancy? Any of these will do you justice. The choice is yours."

When it came down to it Elizabeth was entirely unsure. Her mother, without exception, made all the final decisions for grand occasions. This was not at all like choosing a dress suitable for work. She went pale and wavered. Jensen was beside her in a moment. "Glass of water, please! Sit here... take a moment."

Eventually, she steeled herself and appealed to Jensen for his choice. He shrugged. "But I don't know your tastes. I do have a few tricks in design I use when people are not sure of their preferences. Perhaps we can eliminate some of these with a few choices. Shall we try that?"

She really didn't know what he meant but nodded anyway.

"Okay... lots of flounces in the skirt or just a few?"

A few.

"Fine lace or the simpler tatting?"

Simpler.

"Beading or no beading?"

No beading.

"High neckline or low neckline?"

Somewhere in between.

"Short sleeves or long?"

Short.

The attendant had tossed a number of garments to the side. The lady went back to the Frown Pile and rummaged through it pulling out a rejected garment and wordlessly added it to the Nod Pile.

"Here you are Elizabeth… you have streamlined your choices to these three gowns. You can try them on again if you would like."

She chose the previously rejected one and tried it on. She looked in the tall bevelled mirror and nodded. She would not shame her groom in this gown. She dared not guess at the price tag. She wondered how many months of her housekeeping allowance it would take to pay this off. They fitted slippers, ordered a new crinoline and a very simple veil – all to be delivered tomorrow morning.

5.

Buchanan pulled up the carriage, the horses stamping in their harness, and he loaded their trunks. Jensen held out his hand as Elizabeth seated herself. Then Glennie climbed in all bustle and fuss.

"See. All very proper Miss Elizabeth. Glennie will be accompanying us. She will be here if you need any help." Jensen smiled slightly as if he was amused for the first time in a long while.

She stared at him and then at Glennie and then out the window. She was not sure what he meant. Evidently, he anticipated she would need help and had no confidence in her housekeeping after all. She didn't mind. She would change his mind. He would see that she was not a waste; that she was capable. She survived Madsen and his shop. How hard could keeping house be?

They went passed the boundaries of the city and stopped at the roadside inn of a small town. While Buchanan attended the horses and stabled them, Jensen took Elizabeth to the dining room. "I am hungry, and Glennie prefers to eat with her husband, so we will dine separately."

"Yes Sir," she said compliantly. He said nothing but just raised his brow. She took a deep breath and reminded herself. "Jensen. Jensen." He nodded and pulled out her chair and waited for her to sit. This was very odd. But of course, he would convey the proper display of decorum as if he was in the company of a real lady. It felt nice anyway.

She wondered what it would have been like if Bill had been that way with her. How wonderful it would have been if he had acknowledged her in public! What if he had held open the door, or helped her step up into a buggy, or pulled out her chair? She blushed as the pictures came to a screeching halt. What really happened was that he strode ahead, and she tagged along, pushing through doors to catch up. "Modern women don't expect all that stuff," she could imagine him saying, as his handsome face grinned at her. Perhaps what he meant was that she was strong enough to be self-sufficient, or that he was totally self-absorbed, and she had to make up the difference. She blushed again.

Jensen handed her a menu. "That is a very pretty look, Miss Elizabeth. What might you be thinking about?"

"Bill," and then she gasped. How did he do that? How did he get her to answer even before she meant to? "I mean…"

"Hmm." He picked up his menu and barely looked at it. He put it to the side. "I like the straightforward meals. I'll order the beef."

She looked at him curiously. "You don't seem like a straightforward sort of person. Why do you choose boring food?" She somehow felt daring and wondered how he would handle such frankness.

He had picked up the napkin and then put it down beside his menu and smiled amused. The distraction was a relief. "So, you think my choice of food reflects my character?"

"Oh no, I wouldn't presume…"

"No accusation of presumption is made. But you did just say that you thought my choice of food is boring and that is inconsistent with who you think I am. I find that intriguing." Increasingly she was more than he expected.

"Perhaps you choose straightforward food because other parts of your life are not straight forward."

"Well, Miss Elizabeth, your powers of observation are quite astute: It seems the sensible thinking is coming back. Still, regardless of what it seems, I am a simple man and my preferences are simple."

"You have not chosen simple when it comes to marrying me. This is quite complicated."

"Hmm. You may be right once again." He pointed towards her menu. "You haven't yet told me what you want to order."

She looked down the list and felt the queasiness starting to rise. "Just the omelette I think." She glanced over as Joe and Glennie came into the dining room laughing and joking. "They seem more like good friends than a married couple."

"I'm guessing friendship is not one of those qualities you have been privy to when observing marriages." He had witnessed how her parents were together.

"I never thought it was necessary. I thought that if you were in love then that was enough. But it seems that to talk like a friend with your husband would be a very lovely thing."

"Hence you are missing your Bill." He signalled to the attendant and placed their order.

"Maybe…" She thought that she was missing that they weren't like that at all and she wished they had been. Elizabeth looked at him then, sitting across from her engrossed in the menu he had picked up again as intently as if it was a captivating novel. She realised that she had never really had the time to study the face of this man who had lost so much and yet would offer to save her situation… even probably her life. He was tall and angular; his thick hair was dark and swept back off his face. His nose was large, almost hooked; his jawline gaunt; but his eyes… his eyes were green flecked with brown, and they seemed to see right through her… in a thoughtful way. This man was kind. And it was the most unusual quality for her to place on a man's character because he was certainly not weak. He had voluntarily faced her mother and had not returned shredded and bleeding. That in itself was telling.

Elizabeth picked up the menu again and looked

through the meals. If she had worked at the wayside inn in Farthing, she may have learnt to cook some of these dishes.

"Did you want to order something else?"

"Oh no…" and she hastily put it down.

"It is okay if you do."

"I was just looking at the menu. I always liked the idea of cooking, but I never got to do that. My mother decided where I was to work, and of course, she chose the most influential name available in town. If there had been an opening at the Mayor's office, she would have chosen that. I wanted to work at the stagecoach inn. They had a kitchen like this one."

"That sounds a little messy and not very glamorous."

"Mother thought so. But she never accounted that working with stockfeed and saddles was anything but glamorous as well. It never made sense to me."

"It usually only makes sense if it serves a purpose. What was your purpose in wanting to work in a kitchen?"

"Cooking… and helping people take a break with good food and drink. I have a painting of a little French café at home. I thought the inn was the closest thing that Farthing had to that. I wanted to cook for people as they take a break… to refresh and help them… relate. Like this."

"This?" He stared across as a waitress knocked a tray in her hand and some plates went flying. Someone swore at her as she quickly tried to mop it up. "It is hard to picture you doing something this menial."

"Is that a black mark against me Mr Harker? Does it bother you that I am not ambitious enough? It was my greatest flaw in my mother's eyes."

"No. I don't think it is a blemish on your character to acknowledge you like cooking. It is not unreasonable to suppose that the things we enjoy can seem messy to those around us, especially if they don't understand. I like design. I am an architect."

Elizabeth laughed. "That actually sounds very clean and not messy at all!"

He stared at her smile as if he was seeing something quite remarkable. "Perhaps it is or perhaps it is messy because others do not understand why I bother to do it at all. Some find it puzzling that I haven't just chosen to live off the combined income of my inheritance and my wife's fortune. To me, it serves a purpose. I work, not so much because I have to… but because I love the idea of creating something that wasn't there before. I like being able to design a place to be safe, functional, practical, as well as comfortable and attractive. There are so many elements that come together to make a space like that. And poor design annoys me. See this dining room. The workers have to come from the kitchen, which is way out the back. It makes the service slow and I assume our meals will be cold. If the kitchen was closer… the staff would not get so tired, the meals would be hotter, customers not so grumpy; the flow on makes for a happier world."

She laughed. "I had no idea you were so serious about things other than avoiding dances."

"I imagine there is a lot that we will get to learn about each other Miss Elizabeth."

She started to say something and then stopped.

"What?" he asked as he signalled for a waiter again.

"Oh. Well. I wanted to ask something, but I don't want to appear ungrateful."

"Ahh, the fear of presumption again. I have a policy that you can always ask. I'll promise not to judge you for ingratitude. I'll do what I can if I think it is reasonable enough."

"Oh. Well... I wondered... would it be possible to try what I like doing? Like you said? I've always wanted to cook. But I never did learn. I wondered... well, do you think... only when I have done my other work of course... could I ask Glennie to teach me some dishes... the ones that you like?" She said it with a rush, like she was asking for an extravagant gown. In fact, in her experience, the request for an expensive gown would be generally, more liberally received.

He looked at her soberly, and her face flushed, and she ducked her head. "Please forgive me. It was bold and unnecessary."

"I think it was bold and completely necessary."

"You do?" She looked up surprised.

"Of course. How can I possibly know what you like if you don't talk about it? I am stunned that this has been your life. It is a shame that you have never felt at liberty to say what you think."

"Mr Harker, you are a very unusual man."

He shrugged. "Being accused of being unusual is not new to me... mostly because of my height, or my nose, or the fact that I choose to work at what interests me, or that I'm not a fan of dancing. Unusual is generally acceptable to me."

"Why did you even go to the dance? It is evident that you didn't want to be there."

"Well, Miss Elizabeth, that is a very good question. I regretted it the moment I stepped inside... and hence why I stayed outside. Perhaps I was there just to meet you." He looked at her across the table, and this time she did blush under his gaze; a pretty flush that ran up into her cheeks. He drank some of his red wine and wondered how this would work. This was not what he expected. Not at all. "Sounds like I am going to get the opportunity to taste-test some of these not very boring, not straightforward, dishes after all."

6.

They left early in the morning and travelled most of the day with frequent stops. Buchanan said it was to rest the horses, but Elizabeth had seen Glennie conspiring with him and wondered if it was to break the trip, or even to treat themselves to a holiday tour. They seemed in the best of spirits and it gave a festive feel to their travels. Glennie even sat with Joe on the top seat for some of the legs, leaving just the two of them in the carriage. In many ways it was awkward, but she noticed that Mr Harker was always attentive and kind. She wondered if all his staff would take such liberties, but Mr Harker didn't seem disturbed by any thought that they were taking advantage of his good nature. He went along with their claims that the horses were tired, walking with Elizabeth at their various stops, amiably allowing her to chat about what ever came to mind.

It was just on evening when they pulled into the driveway of a Beachside Cottage that the family used as a holiday retreat. Glennie and Joe chattered and laughed while they unloaded their trunks and bags. Glennie only allowed Elizabeth to carry the lighter items, but even so, it didn't take long to have it all stowed into their allocated rooms.

Elizabeth woke to the sound of waves and seagulls. She had retired early, wearied from the full day of travel, and she hadn't had much of a look around. She stepped through the French doors to the balcony. She looked out over the beach, flushed with dawn pink across the sky, and she watched as it melted through a palette of pastel colours as the sun rose over the ocean.

"Good morning, Miss Elizabeth…"

"Oh! Good morning Sir." She clutched the dressing-gown covering her nightdress a little closer. She had no idea their rooms adjoined the same verandah.

"Are you normally an early riser?"

"No Sir. Not usually." She felt groggy from sleep, but it seemed bizarre to her that, as yet, she had not lifted one duster or one broom. "I wanted to see what routines needed attending to this morning."

He nodded thoughtfully. "Today I have the most important undertaking to attend to. Not routine."

"Oh yes, Sir. Whatever you need."

"I need you to be dressed in your gown and ready to leave at half-past nine. Glennie will help you. The church is booked for ten o'clock. We will have a photograph taken afterwards."

"Today, Sir? The church? To be married? Today?"

"Today."

The church was stark; the priest was formal; the ceremony short. Glennie was in her best dress, and Joe signed as the witness. The photographer positioned them for a portrait, and then it was over.

When they returned to the house, Jensen removed his cravat and sat in the lounge while Glennie prepared a very fine lunch. He even insisted that Glennie and Joe eat with them when she brought out the dishes. It was a silent meal contrasting to the amiable chatting of the day before. Then, quite unapologetically, Jensen excused himself after lunch for a nap. He said that he found these types of extraordinary endeavours exhausting. "My apologies, Elizabeth, you will have to amuse yourself for a couple of hours. Possibly read a book? Perhaps we could walk on the beach when I get up?"

She nodded, relieved, and Glennie helped her undress out of her gown. For once she was not chatty or nosy and quietly excused herself after hanging the gown to the side of the dresser. Elizabeth sat on the bed in her petticoat and looked at it for some time. Eventually, she retired with a book, but it very quickly slid out of her hand. When she woke, she picked the volume up off the floor and dressed in the same dark blue dress she had worn in the library. She stepped outside onto the balcony bathed in afternoon shadows.

Jensen was sitting in a chair reading. He adjusted his round glasses. "I hope I didn't disturb you. I have not long got up." He went to pour himself a cup of tea, but the pot was empty. He put it back down beside his book.

Elizabeth looked at the cold cup of tea on the tray beside him and nothing seemed like he had just crawled out of bed. "No Sir... I was not disturbed, not at all. You said you wanted to walk on the beach. I only remember one holiday as a child. It was winter and windy, so all my dreams of seaside holidays are a little tainted with memories of very chilly sand-storms."

He tilted his head, almost amused. "That doesn't sound terribly pleasant, which means the standard is not too high to avoid disappointment. It is not windy this afternoon, so why don't we give it a try?"

They walked over the dunes together, the sound of the waves creating a backdrop to their silence.

Jensen stopped at an outcrop of rocks and sat down. "I think I will take my boots off. I find sand tenacious once it gets in the leather stitching. Are you brave enough to try that yourself, Mrs Elizabeth?"

She jolted. Mrs? Oh. She supposed that was true. "Barefoot? Outside?"

He looked around cautiously at the empty shoreline and shrugged carelessly. "There is no one here to judge us. Why not?"

She raised her brow and undid her laces and slid off her stockings tucking them into her shoes. She stepped out onto the sand. Her face seemed quite incredulous, but it was more the idea that he was not scandalised that had her wondering. She explored the firmness of the wet sand, tentatively lifting her skirts to allow the foam of the small waves to wash around her toes.

"So how does it feel?"

"Oh wonderful!" she said spontaneously.

He nodded and smiled. "I meant being Mrs... Mrs Elizabeth Harker."

"Oh."

"Perhaps it is just exploring the awareness of something new."

"Yes Sir, that is it exactly. It is very new."

"And what about the beach?"

"This is new too. But I think it is very enjoyable without the wind." They walked on for a time. Every so often Elizabeth would pick up a shell and marvel at the pattern and shape and colour and shine. "Mr Harker?"

"Jensen. Hmm?"

"Mr Jensen... what do your daughters think about you getting married?"

He stopped walking and looked at her. "Actually, they do not know. We had to leave quickly and given your mother's prohibition on any communication of the wedding; I find myself in an unusual dilemma."

"Your daughters don't know? Oh, Sir, this is not good!"

He frowned thoughtfully. At least she appreciated this was a delicate situation. He was surprised that she expected him to have an open and loving bond with his daughters, even though her own relationship with her parents revolved around rules and expectations and status. "I think I have finally found something on which I can I agree with your Bill. You are a modern thinker Mrs Elizabeth. Many don't value a father's responsibility to their daughters, yet my girls mean everything to me. I told them I was going away for a month. I said that when I get back we would talk. It distresses me that I have needed to do this without their knowledge or consent."

"Consent?"

"I think it is important to have the agreement of the people we love if at all possible." Even as he said it, he knew in this situation such an ideal was a virtual fantasy. There were people who would never understand. He prayed his daughters were not included in that number.

"If possible…" she agreed with a frown. "But Sir, what if your daughters do not agree? Glennie said your wife died so suddenly, so tragically. They must be still so very sad."

"We all are… yes…"

"Oh, Sir. I am so sorry."

"I have been thinking about this a lot… very little else actually. No slight intended against my bride of course. It is going to be difficult to tell them. But perhaps it is realistic for you to be aware that you may not be welcomed with open arms."

"Oh Sir, I think they will understand since I am not really your wife."

"What do you mean? You really are my wife. We have a certificate to prove it."

"Well, you know… more just being your housekeeper."

He pursed his lips thoughtfully. "Hmm. That is one way to consider this. But in actuality, I think it would be preferable that everyone believes this is a complete marriage: bedroom and all. And that they believe that your baby… is my baby: our honeymoon baby."

"You are willing to let everyone think this is your baby?"

"I think it would be best. In fact, I insist."

"But Sir, that is not going to be terribly convincing when we sleep in separate situations."

"A dilemma indeed. Perhaps we need to get used to 'one' situation then."

She stopped, and her eyes went dark and her mouth dropped open. She gasped and ran off down the beach. He watched her go and walked along the edge of the water, the wet sand impressed by his tread, deep in thought. He came across her sitting on a log of driftwood half-buried in the sand. He looked at her face wet with tears and sat down beside her.

"What has upset you Elizabeth?"

"You know what has upset me. You promised! You promised that you would not expect the bedroom. And yet the wedding day is not even over, and you are already breaking your promise. I thought you were different! I thought you would be a man of your word."

"Oh." He looked out across the waves and felt the tumble of his life being swirled around like driftwood in the surf. "I apologise for the misunderstanding. When I said the bedroom 'duties' of a wife, I meant making love, not where we sleep."

She gasped and blushed a deep red.

"Elizabeth, you are a child. I am not going to make love with a child of sixteen, whether she is pregnant or not."

"I am not a child!" she said defensively. "I've already done that. Obviously."

"Were you not just crying, because you thought you would be subjected to the wifely duties of the bedroom?"

"Well yes. But that is because you promised I wouldn't have to."

"It is a promise I intend to keep. Even though you doubt it, I am a man of my word. We are married, and even if at some point you would like that bedroom rule to change Elizabeth, not until you are eighteen.

Minimum. That is my rule."

"Eighteen? So, I will have to when I am eighteen?"

"No. You won't have to. You will never 'have to'. That is something that both adults want to do. Not one over the other."

"So, I don't have to... ever?" It was a weight off her shoulders. She was released. The idea of that... with someone so old... just seemed beyond unpleasant.

"So, you are my wife. But that is all. However, the entire civilized world needs to believe that this marriage is consummated. The easiest way for that to happen is for everyone to understand that this baby is mine." He picked up a stick and wrote in the sand. "Even my daughters must believe it."

"I'm pretty sure Glennie knows. She saw me be sick and then she brought me tea and dry toast."

"Glennie is discreet and loyal... for all her chatting. I trust her. She probably thinks that in a moment of need, a moment of comfort, this baby is mine. Hence why we have married so quickly."

She gasped and blushed again. How could he not be embarrassed to talk about these things? "So, you want us to share the same bedroom? How are we going to do that?"

"After the baby is born you might like to sleep in the nursery for a while. But otherwise... my bed is your bed. We may need to practise, that is all."

"Practise?"

"Yes. So we are used to being there. Together."

"Sir, I don't think I can."

"You can because we need to."

"Oh, this is complicated! I should have just gone to the poorhouse."

"No doubt there will be times when you'll wish you had opted for that. We will get used to it."

That evening as they got ready for bed, Elizabeth blushed and sighed and procrastinated. Eventually, Jensen, in his nightshirt and dressing gown turned down the covers for her and she climbed in. She lay there stiff as a board. "Good night Elizabeth. Sleep well."

"I doubt it, Sir." She took a deep breath

He nodded, leant over and kissed her on the forehead, and she squeezed her eyes shut. He picked up a candle and went downstairs.

After about half an hour Elizabeth appeared at the library door in her nightdress with a candle. He looked up and saw her there. "Are you not coming to bed, Sir?"

"I am not. I thought I would wait until you were asleep."

"But I was waiting for you."

"I was attending to some reading; I didn't want to disturb you."

"I am already disturbed. I can't get used to you if you are not there to get used to."

"Oh. Well, I suppose that is true."

"You could read in the chair by the glass doors in the room… if that was agreeable."

He frowned. "You want me there while you fall asleep?" It sounded like Eunice demanding the presence of her nursery maid.

"Just until I get used to you. Please, Sir. This is very awkward. I am trying."

"Hmm. Yes. Awkward it is. And… what you ask does not seem unreasonable. So, I will try also." He snapped his book shut and picked up his reading lamp.

He settled into the chair in the corner and corrected the light of the lamp while Elizabeth adjusted her bedcovers. She fussed and pummelled her pillow. And then lay there… with her eyes closed… with her eyes open, closed, open. "You know Sir… I never imagined that this is what my wedding day would be like. As a little girl, I used to pretend with my friends all the things we would do and have… and never in my wildest dreams did I think it would be like this."

Jensen nodded, and then went back to finding his place in his book.

"I think the thing that surprises me the most is not having my mother there. I always thought I would look so pretty and make her so proud because she always talked about how it would be a relief to see me married in a suitable situation. I guess that is why I thought that Bill would… you know… be a suitable husband, because Mother had pursued that position at the agency so doggedly. Still, I find it a very odd turn of phrase: 'Suitable'. It sounds like a pair of shoes or a waist-coat... not a marriage."

He looked up and sighed, then quietly placed a bookmark in the chapter.

"What is unexpected though, is that even without her arrangement or approval, I really do have the most suitable marriage. And she doesn't even know, or care, or could be bothered... and it hurts that she thinks that it is more fun to be in mourning over me disappearing, than to be at my wedding. It is a very strange way to look at your family. I would never want that. If we have a daughter, I will never want that for her. I am very sure you would never want that for your daughters. I would want to be there I think... even if I got it in my head... that somehow it was not suitable..."

Jensen went to put his book down on the side-table until he realised that Elizabeth was breathing regularly in sleep. He looked at her asleep on Georgina's pillow innocently unaware of the pain it brought him to see her there.

7.

Elizabeth woke to the sound of the waves and stepped out onto the balcony. Jensen was reading his book. "You don't sleep much, do you Sir," she observed as she rubbed her eyes.

"I slept adequately thank you." In truth, he dozed in the chair and then slept on top of the covers awkwardly aware of the unrelenting sense of betrayal pounding him like the surf in the background. "Yourself? Did you sleep well?"

"Oh yes, thank you, Sir. I seem to be so tired I could sleep on a rock."

"Growing babies is an exhausting business. My wife used to say that."

"I wish she was here, Sir. I think she could have taught me a lot. I don't know much about babies. Oh." She saw the pained looked that crossed his face. "Oh! I am so sorry Sir. Of course, if she was here I wouldn't be allowed to talk to her!" She turned and ran inside.

Jensen made no move to follow her but looked out towards the beach. How many times, countless times, had Georgina waved to him, as he sat reading his books here on this balcony? She would hold her broad-brimmed hat in her hand and her windswept face would glow with laughter as she was returning from her morning walk on the beach. When he came down later to breakfast, he found Glennie in the kitchen. "Where is Elizabeth?"

"I believe that she is outside Mr Jensen." She seemed reluctant to say anything further and returned to kneading her bread with uncharacteristic focus.

He went for a wander, down the front stairs and along the path towards the beach. He swept his gaze across the shoreline and didn't see her, so walked back to the house. He heard her humming as he turned around the side of the house. He stood and watched Elizabeth scrubbing clothes at the laundry copper, rinsing the dripping garments and running them through the mangle. Her hair was damp and there was a bubble of suds on her temple where she had tucked her hair behind her ear. She looked up and jolted.

"Oh! Good morning, Sir."

"We said good morning earlier..."

"Yes, Sir, we did."

"Jensen. Please. Call me Jensen." He indicated the washing board. "You have made an early start."

She indicated a nail under the house where a wooden hanger was holding her wedding gown, the hem and train protected from the ground by sheets and towels. "It needs to be washed immediately, even though I did not wear it for very long yesterday. Once it has dripped dry I will take it upstairs so that it can finish drying inside. I will need to find a hook high enough to take the length so that it doesn't dry scrunched. It is so beautiful that I want it to stay in the

70

very best condition."

"Oh."

"And since I was here, there were some other laundry items from travelling that I thought I could do."

"Hmm. You sound very proficient when it comes to these matters. It does not seem like the first time you have attended to this Elizabeth."

She looked a little snubbed. "Does it surprise you, Sir, that I can actually do housekeeping? Life at Farthing was not at all like Mrs Grissom's Ball. It was much more… basic. That was a constant frustration for my mother."

"I guess I assumed that the only daughter of Mrs Edwina Perkins might be a little pampered."

"If that was your assumption, Sir, then you took quite a gamble in having me as your housekeeper."

"Seems it is one that will pay off." He stared at the pile of clothes. "Finish up here Elizabeth, and when you are done come and see me in the Library."

She swiped back her hair again and curtsied. "Of course, Sir."

When she came in he was settled into his chair, with a pot of tea by his side. He indicated for her to sit and he closed his book. "Did you find a suitable hook high enough on which to hang your dress?"

"I did. Glennie got Joe to hang it up for me in the spare room just by the robe. There happens to be a hook in the ceiling that is perfect. Sir, did you ask

Joe to install it just now?"

He smiled slightly and shrugged as he poured a cup without asking and pushed it towards her. He glanced around the room. "I have been building this library for many years. It is my holiday pleasure... reading. Do you like to read Miss... Mrs Elizabeth?"

"I really don't know Sir. I did well at school, but I never did read just for the sake of it. It always seemed like homework, Sir."

"Perhaps you have not found the right sort of books. I bought Georgina some recently published novels that you might read."

"What for, Sir?"

"What do you mean, "what for"?"

"We only read at school to write an essay."

"Well, it is a way to think about new ideas... learn things. You said earlier you don't know much about being a mother. If you are not interested in stories, perhaps you can read those sorts of books."

"You have books about babies Sir? That seems a little odd."

"Odd?"

"Well, yes... odd. Don't you think it is odd for someone who is old to have books about babies?"

"How old do you think I am Elizabeth?"

"Oh, I don't know... fifty..." She shrugged. "Fifty-five? Sixty?"

"You are going up?"

"Well Sir, you are... old."

"Just for the record, I am forty-two."

"See. That is very old."

"Noted; although I didn't ask you to come here to discuss my seniority. There are some routines that are part of our family that I expect you to start to participate in. One of those is that we eat our meals together, including breakfast, and also a walk on the beach in the evening. It is a holiday routine that I prefer. So, when you are organising your day, please work around that. The rest of the time is pretty much yours to do what you want. When I go back to the firm there will be a different routine of course."

"The firm – that is where you work?"

"It is. Right in the city... I generally have Buchannan drive me. It allows time to observe and gives me the creative space that commuting in other ways does not allow. Once I get to the office it is very busy."

"Huh. Everything in your life is very intentional Sir. It seems that you don't do anything just on the moment."

"Perhaps some would challenge that my lack of spontaneity has taken a turn just recently," he suggested with a faint smile.

"Not me. Even when you change what you were going to do, you do it for a reason."

"Is that so? What do you mean?"

"Well... like the shopping Sir. You already said that you didn't do shopping if you can help it, but you went with me to buy my dress. I think you changed your mind because you didn't trust me to get something proper because I would think it too expensive."

"What you chose was very suitable for a bride: it was beautiful and flattering."

"It was very kind Sir. And generous. Of course, I expect you to deduct the cost of my gown from my allowance... but if you could do it over a period of time that would be appreciated, because although I don't actually know how much it was, I do know it was very expensive."

He looked at her and his face that had stayed almost expressionless up to this point melted into a grin with a shake of his head. "Well, now it is my turn to think you are odd."

"Oh. Really? Is that bad? I don't mean to..."

"Elizabeth I am not going to make you pay for your wedding dress as if it is a debt. It was something for our wedding day. I think you have very low expectations of me as your husband. By the way, there is a book about raising children on that bookshelf over there. Grey cover. Yes. Have a look at it and perhaps you can tell me what you think tomorrow."

"Yes, Sir. Ah, I mean... Mr... Jensen?"
"Hmm?"

"Is there any particular thing about housekeeping you want me to do? You haven't talked about that at all. It is very strange."

"Why is it strange? You said you can do it, and the evidence is that you are an expert at the mangle, so why would I want to tell you how to do your job?"

"Oh... I hadn't thought of it like that."

"Perhaps you are worried about when your allowance will start?"

"Oh no. I wasn't asking about that. I wouldn't presume."

"It's not presumption if we have already agreed to it. It'll be the standard rate for housekeeping. I pay on the fortnight. Is that okay?"

"Whatever you think is reasonable Sir."

"I think it is. Lunch is at noon, and as it is already close you might as well stay here. Perhaps you can look at your book."

"Sir, when you are at home, not here, but when we go back... are your meals... well, do you want me there... or do you dine alone?

"Of course, you will be there. I expect the same of my daughters."

"And... when the baby is born, will that be... like... um..."

"You are wondering whether the baby will be treated with the same expectations as my other daughters?"

She nodded, her cheeks flushing.

"Well given she is my baby... our honeymoon baby... I think that would apply. Don't you?"

"I wasn't sure Sir."

"Please just…" He let it ride but wondered how much stamina he had to insist she use his name.

At dinner, they sat down at the dining room table. "So, Elizabeth, how is it that you are comfortable with a mangle and yet don't know how to cook? It is an unusual oversight of your mother."

"I'm not really sure Sir, except Mother was fanatical about fashion and thought it was important to understand how to wash the fabrics appropriately. She could never trust anyone else to do it well. She said she had a couple of very fine gowns spoilt by incompetence. Cooking was less interesting for her perhaps… and we had a good cook."

"So, you had a good cook, and yet you never learnt?"

"Eating food doesn't mean you can prepare it well. I tried a couple of times to sneak into the kitchen, but our cook was very territorial. Mother preferred it that way."

That night Elizabeth took less time to get ready for bed. She slid into bed and stayed close to the edge. "Are you going to read tonight Sir?"

"I believe so. I am at a very interesting part of my book."

"Oh." She sat up and took her own book off the table near the bed. She paused as she opened the cover. "Sir, do you think it is acceptable to disagree with something that is in a book? I mean… to write a book would require such great learning so part of me considers that it must be true. It's just that I would find it very hard to believe every single thing that is in a book. After all, what is in one book could very well contradict another book. I was reading this and the recommendations in this book all seem very harsh. Although I would be reluctant to disagree whole-heartedly with such published wisdom, I just wondered… is it possible to consider imprudent what others consider wise? Mother would say this is the foolishness of youth speaking… and I know I am young, but you Sir, you are not young and you are very intentional and thoughtful person… and I wondered what you thought about that."

Jenson sort of blinked in the lamplight and adjusted his glasses. He had not expected such an outpouring of doubt. "Elizabeth, learning is not just accepting and retaining facts. It is also being able to weigh their value. Have you read something that you don't quite agree with?"

"Well, this book has a list of very common sort of manners associated with being a mother. Just here it says, *"it is very unladylike to speak to or of a gentleman by their first name unless you are related to them"*. And I know that now I am married, that makes me related, but it does seem a little strange that your request three days ago is rude and today it is acceptable, even if it is just in private."

"Just because it is in print, doesn't make it a universal truth. A piece of writing is the author's opinion. I think it is admirable that you are considering things for yourself."

"And this one says that using my imagination is exposing me to great risk: "*laying a foundation of hysterical, hypochondriacal, and even maniacal diseases*". Sir – how can that be so? Earlier they said a child with imagination is commended, so how can something that was good a couple of pages ago, now subject me to madness? Even as a child I am still the same person I am now." He smiled, and she blushed and put down her book. "Oh, Sir you are laughing at me. I am sorry to bother you."

"Don't be ridiculous Elizabeth. I smile, not because you are foolish, but because I don't often hear such sense, even from people who are twice your age. Don't give up on challenging conventional wisdom. It may be accepted as very sensible, but just because someone says it is so in a book, doesn't necessarily mean it is. I think you have asked some very good questions."

"Then why do you consider reading so worthy? It just seems confusing."

"Well, there is a maxim that says reading is 'food for thought'. You would like to cook to make something delicious, to make our bodies strong. Reading is cooking for our minds. You've reflected on things you wouldn't normally do so just by reading that book, even if their logic is weak."

"Do you think that is okay Sir? For a woman to

think about such things?"

"I am surrounded by beautiful women whom I encourage to do the same. My daughters are wilful thinkers also."

At that, she chuckled and settled down in the bed. "That must make your life provoking Sir. You don't make it easy on yourself."

"And yet it delivers something that is generally more valuable to me than 'easy'." He opened his book and tried to focus back on his reading. Elizabeth turned onto her side and lay there for a while studying his face in the yellow glow of his reading lamp, and before long she was breathing regularly in sleep.

8.

They walked along the beach in bare feet. This was a holiday ritual that Elizabeth looked forward to. A month had gone by in a predictable unvaried routine. She had hoped to try cooking, but the smells overwhelmed her with waves of nausea, so it was not practical. Glennie reassured her that it would eventually settle down and she could try again then. During the day she spent a lot of time resting and used that time to read. It had not taken long to review her short life, and Jensen, although a great listener, was not a prolific talker, so reading became fodder for subjects to talk about during their afternoon beachside strolls. Jensen insisted most of the housekeeping be left to Glennie because this was their honeymoon, even in name, and indicated that she would resume her duties once they returned home.

Elizabeth focused on the horizon where a blurry haze made it almost impossible to distinguish where the ocean started, and sky finished. "How did your daughters take the news, Sir?" She hoped very much that her voice sounded casual.

Jensen walked on in silence. He tried to construct his words in a way that wouldn't be outright upsetting. To say the girls had 'not taken it well' would be sanitising what really happened. They had been so excited to see him when he arrived, and they sat outside after they returned from church with tea and damper. They were busily chatting about their holiday news: horse riding adventures, encounters with farm animals, and escapades with their cousins. It was such a relief to see them relaxed and smiling. Being away from the expectations of society seemed to promote a balance he wanted to encourage. Finally, Susanna paused, and Jensen took a deep breath knowing he could procrastinate no longer. "I have some very important news. It affects us all."

He had their attention immediately. "Is it good news?"

"I hope so..." had been his reflex response, and he quickly tried to regain his composure with his rehearsed speech. "It has been a difficult time for all of us since Mama's accident. I confess I have neglected you as we adjust to our terrible loss. I have resolved to look after myself better so that I will be an improved father for you. So... I have decided to marry again. She is young and well mannered. I hope we will all get along."

"You're getting married?" they exclaimed in unison.

"Well... actually... I already am. This time I have been away has been our honeymoon; there is a standard four weeks to start married life. We have needed this time to adjust to our new lives."

"You can't be married! Why have you forgotten Mama so soon! What about her? I never thought you would betray her like this!" Susanna stood up so abruptly that the garden chair fell backwards.

"Elizabeth will come home with me in about two weeks. At the moment she is not very well and cannot travel comfortably."

Susanna stood there glaring at her father and then she picked up the pitcher of lemon-water on the table and tossed it all over their afternoon tea, splashing it down the front of his Sunday suit. "I hate you!" she screamed as she stormed away towards the stables.

Eunice looked at her sister leave, her eyes wide in shock, and then stared at her father. She quickly got up and fled to the house in tears.

Jensen cleared his throat again and looked down at Elizabeth who was intently studying a shell, wiping the colours with her finger wet with seawater. "Well, I do know they didn't want to celebrate this news by writing polite welcome letters."

Elizabeth dropped the shell and looked hard at his face. She guessed what that meant. Eventually, she turned away. "It is like you are a prophet, Sir. You said that they would reject me."

"Just because I know my children well enough to predict their reactions, doesn't mean I desired it or manipulated it. I expect a time of adjustment; that is why I went to tell them yesterday. They need time to think this through. There have been big changes to our world."

When their carriage arrived back at the estate, and Elizabeth was helped down the step holding Jensen's hand, both girls stood near the stairway to formally greet them. They saw her, curtsied and turned to walk inside. Jensen quickly strode out toward his daughters and embraced them both. Elizabeth observed intently to see what family loyalties would prevail. They were children after all. Who could blame him when they had not long lost their beloved Mama? He guided them both firmly back to where Elizabeth stood. "Elizabeth, may I introduce to you, two of the most accomplished and beautiful young ladies around. This is Susanna and Eunice. Girls, this is Elizabeth, my new wife."

They curtsied formally to each other and Elizabeth felt faint as she rose, and she wobbled ungainly. Jensen quickly supported her, and they made their way inside. Elizabeth retired soon after, exhausted.

In the morning they were sitting at the table waiting to start breakfast when Elizabeth cleared her throat and begged pardon to ask a question in a low whisper. Jensen looked at her expectantly. "Sir, I wondered when you might consider it time to tell your daughters..."

"Tell us what?" said Susanna without ceremony as they walked through the door for breakfast. Eunice appeared behind her sister wide-eyed and sulky.

Elizabeth jolted and blushed, ducking her head. Jenson considered her for a moment and turned to his daughters. "Well…" he paused and swallowed. "We were going to wait a little longer until we could be sure. But why not? We think Elizabeth may be pregnant. She is expecting a baby."

"Oh, you have got to be kidding me," sighed Susanna in a world-weary tone.

"No," said Jensen patiently. "We are not teasing. Of course, it is not confirmed yet because we have only been married six weeks so it would be appreciated if you didn't tell anyone as yet. Sometimes pregnancies do not last, and this may be the case. This is just our family news for now." He affectionately reached out and held Elizabeth's hand and just ever so slightly he felt her wince under his touch. He didn't blink but smiled at his daughters and said gently. "A baby is very happy news."

Happy news? After breakfast, Elizabeth went for a walk around the Estate. She had never thought of this baby as happy news. She wondered if he meant it or whether it was part of the pretending. This news had been uncertain, hopeful, frightening, horrifying… but not happy. It had never been happy. What would it be like to think of this baby as happy news? She sat down in a little garden alcove with a small outside setting and thought about that. Why couldn't it also be happy? Why couldn't this be the family she had dreamt of as a child? That is where the picture came to a screeching halt. All her romantic imaginings as a child were not just happy and energetic; they were also romantic and full of kisses and love. She noticed the darkness of a deep sadness. She was not here as a woman in love. She was here as a housekeeper and that meant she needed Jensen to be reassured she could do his housekeeping well. She took a deep breath. Her mother had wanted her out of the way. Well, she was out. Elizabeth had found an unexpected path to survival and she was not going to just survive. Her plan was also to flourish. Her and her baby… and if it was possible… her new family.

She stood up and took herself on a tour of the estate house. It was large and spacious, and she set about exploring every room. What a place! The focal point of downstairs was Jensen's library. The staircase was wide and the rooms upstairs extensive. She thought about the little book that had been her saviour at the little Farthing agency. And she decided that she would like her own little book… a place where she could write notes. She knocked at the door of the library. "Excuse me, Sir…"

Jensen quickly looked up and indicated for her to come in. "Elizabeth," he said quietly, "family does not use formal designations like 'Sir'. I really must insist that you try to remember that. It is important."

Elizabeth jolted. *Family?* Had he read her thoughts? His correction was just another failure, like

Bill telling her to remember all their customer's preferences. She looked at him with tears. "I really don't want to appear disrespectful Sir, and it seems that addressing you so familiarly, is so close to that line. I wish to do what you want of course."

"This is what I want. Now, what is it that *you* wanted?"

"Oh. Well, I wondered where I could buy a book Si..." She stopped herself. There were very few demands Mr Harker insisted on... just this one thing actually. Perhaps if she couldn't call him by his first name, she need not call him anything at all.

"What sort of book are you looking for?" he said looking around at his shelves.

"Not a reading book, but a writing book. Something I could write in."

"You would like to write some correspondence?"

"No Si... No. A book to write notes and information in... housekeeping things. Things I might need to remember..."

"Hmm." He sighed, and then got up and walked over to an elegant writing desk and drew back the roll top. He seemed to freeze for a moment, as he stared at the collection of stationery, inkwell and pen set. There was a small handkerchief trimmed with lace folded to the side. He quickly shut the lid and went over to his large desk and opened a drawer. He pulled out a leather-bound notebook and tore out the first few pages. "I have not used this for a while. Would this meet your needs?" he said gruffly.

She nodded silently. How different his life was from hers. Jensen loved his wife; at every turn, there was a memory of her haunting his world. Did Bill even miss her? She wondered if he regretted his uncompromising stance. She liked to think that he would wander down to the place where they would meet and touch their initials carved into a gumtree there, and smile wistfully for his forsaken love.

"I also wanted to ask… there are some things of mine at my Grandparent's estate where my parents are staying… like my writing set. Is it possible to have them brought here? We left so suddenly."

He sat back down and opened his book. "Of course. I'll send Buchanan over to collect all your things tomorrow," he said into the pages. He looked up impatiently when he realised she hadn't moved. "Yes?"

"Could I borrow a pen until then Si… please?"

He closed his eyes as if rebuking himself. He nodded and went back to his desk and pulled out a small portable writing set, worn and bound in a leather wrap. He handed it to her without a word. She went to say something else, but he held up his hand. He indicated the door and dismissed her.

She swallowed hard and left. She went outside and sat down again at the little white table and chair in the garden alcove. It was comforting that this little setting was tucked away, forgotten, in a corner of the garden; away from Mr Harker; away from the girls; away from her memories of Bill when he was attentive and smooth. She put her head on her arms and felt the weight of her position. Like a flood chute opening, suddenly she was sobbing. Since they had left Farthing, escaping like refugees in the night, she had never allowed her tears to fall. Not like this.

Slowly the flood eased, and she sat up and wiped her face. She told herself she should be grateful. She shouldn't be sad. She shouldn't be anything but blissfully indebted because she was saved from a poorhouse. But she was not wanted here. The girls glared and resented her. Mr Harker tolerated her. He said "family" but meant "servant".

Oh. What was wrong with her? That was exactly what she was. This was her job. She was in service. Slowly, like the mist melting with the heat of the morning sun, she could see this for what it was. This was a position that paid an allowance that was not siphoned off for someone else's good ideas. Here, there was the possibility of opportunities, perhaps more than she ever had at home. This was a place where she could learn new things beyond the confines of that little regional school in Farthing. Here she had received more consideration than she ever was given at Madsen's agency. This relationship offered her more respect than she ever got from Bill or Old Mr Madsen. And it might not be romantic, and it might not look how she imagined her life to look, but the only romantic experience of her short life had broken her heart. She swallowed and resigned herself to the idea that those fleeting couple of heady months was to be her only taste of being courted by a beau. That was it. Short. Intoxicating. Heartbreaking. This situation was everything that was not... complicated, honest, routine. But it was more. Enduring. Sustaining. Healing.

Suddenly this life seemed safer. Jensen never pretended it was more than this. He pretended to other people so they would leave them alone to get on with their lives to survive tragedies that neither of them had desired or sought. That was their common ground. She may never win over the girls, but she would make Jensen see that the caution he had thrown to the wind by taking her in, would not be in vain. His daughters' house would be well kept. That would be the comfort in his grief. She retraced the pain in his eyes she had witnessed as he opened his wife's writing desk. Even without willing it, there developed an ache in her to see him consoled and content once more.

She wiped her eyes and opened her book. Instinctively she smelt the leather binding and was surprised at the lingering fragrance of Jensen's shaving water. She almost smiled as she thought about how she had so confidently sold her housekeeping capabilities. Maybe she could act after all. She conceded she had been a little liberal with her claims of competence. She suspected Jensen probably knew that she didn't know that much, given her age and inexperience, but he hadn't hesitated. His unwavering belief in her gave her courage. She could do what she knew, and she was sure Glennie could teach her what she didn't. She unfolded the writing set and picked up a pen. She opened the cover and at the top of each page she wrote down a room. Underneath that, she listed all the household routines that she thought might be needed, or taken for granted, or forgotten. She prioritised chores that needed doing on their allocated day... and marked off things that would be needed less often. And when she had finished she flicked through the pages and decided where she would start. Yes. Now she had a plan to prove Jensen's belief was well-founded.

9.

After breakfast one day during the week, Elizabeth gathered the dishes and went into the kitchen where Glennie was scrubbing the pots. She propped herself on a stool and looked at Glennie elbow-deep in suds.

"Glennie, how do you like working for Mr Harker?"

She looked at Elizabeth across the bench and wondered at the question. "Well Ma'am, we have worked with him for a long time now... before even Miss Susanna was born, so we are used to each other's ways."

"Do you remember at the Beachside Cottage I asked if you might give me cooking lessons? Maybe we can start our cooking soon? I find it hard to keep on top of all the housekeeping, but I am trying."

Glennie chuckled a little. "Well, I never. You are a strange one for the lady of the house... that is for sure."

"I feel so much better now and I really would like to try cooking. Do you think you could teach me? Something for a Sunday tea perhaps, after church. Since Mr Harker has been back at work I hardly seem to see him. He is very busy."

"That he is Ma'am."

"Glennie, you could call me Elizabeth. Mr

Jensen would not be displeased I am sure."

She glanced up over the sudsy tub filled with saucepans and shook her head. "You are a strange one for sure Ma'am."

Every day Elizabeth went to work, dusting, and wiping and sweeping. Each day she collected items that the girls had discarded on the floor and adjusted linen and curtains and covers. Her work developed a comfortable rhythm as she went around the house, humming a tune on her lips.

One Saturday morning, Susanna came out and stood at the door to her room. "Elizabeth, you have not cleaned my room properly!"

"What do you mean?"

"I mean it is a disgrace. You need to take more care."

"Of course... if you could tell me in what regard. I have not changed..."

"Exactly. You have not changed the curtains. You are lazy and taking advantage of my father's position! You need to scrub all of the..."

"Susanna?"

They froze as Jensen stood at the top of the stairs. His voice was quiet, firm. Susanna looked triumphant as Elizabeth dropped her eyes.

"Yes Father?" she said sweetly.

"Are you concerned about Elizabeth's care of the house?"

"Yes, I am actually. I think that she is sloppy."

"What specifically?"

"Well, the skirting boards for one, and the window sills. The curtains, like I said. The furniture has not been polished in a week, and Mama would never have allowed..."

"Oh. I see. Well, that is disappointing."

"It certainly is!"

"The best solution will be that you now look after your room, and you can also help Eunice with hers."

"What? No! Why should I be punished because she is not doing it well? That is not what I meant at all."

"I think this will be best. I will check tomorrow that it is all done to your exacting standards. Elizabeth, come down to the Library directly. I have something I wish to discuss."

She nodded and murmured, "Of course." And she hurried off to put away the items in her arms.

Jensen turned to go, then paused and looked back at his daughter. "And Susanna, I know there is an adjustment period and I will make allowances, but please do not speak with such disrespect again. There are ways to address concerns without spite. You are not a spiteful person, so be mindful of your tone."

"Yes, Father..." There was smouldering resentment in her lowered gaze.

Elizabeth came into the Library quietly and stood by one of the bookshelves waiting for Jensen to pause in his reading. Her face was flushed, anticipating the reprimand that was coming.

"Come and sit…"

She took a deep breath and braced herself for the scolding. "Yes… Sir."

"Has that happened before?" He didn't look up from what he was reading.

"I do not think so Sir. I always try to do my best. I do not think I have been neglecting the housekeeping. Although I will allow that it is a big house and I may…"

He closed his book. "I mean: are the girls giving you grief like that often?"

"Oh. No Sir. No. Not at all. This has been the only time that there seems to be any dissatisfaction."

He shook his head and pressed his lips. "I thought you were getting better at acting. That was a terrible performance."

"But Sir they are only children! They are distressed about losing their mother. It follows that they are going to find my presence difficult."

"Difficult it can be, without being obnoxious. You have difficult things to adjust to also, yet I don't see you being narky. That can hardly be accounted for by age alone."

She said nothing, yet something quite profound happened inside her. He had defended her… as his wife. "I hope you are pleased with my work."

"Oh goodness, there is nothing wrong with what

you do. That is my point. But I also wanted to check that you are looking after yourself... and our baby. Is everything going well with you? I trust you can come to me if you need to."

Elizabeth sighed. How would she know? She had no one to talk to. Glennie never had children. She missed her holiday talks with Jensen as they walked along the beach or as they retired, and she dozed off to sleep to the rhythmic sound of the waves. Now he was up early to go to the office and Jensen rarely came to their room before she was fast asleep. Sometimes, apart from a ruffled pillowcase, she would have sworn that he slept in the library. He did say that when he was back at work there would be a different routine, but she had not expected things to be so different that they would rarely cross paths. The evening meals were socially strained occasions focused on the girls and their studies or accomplishments.

"Glennie is taking me to meet the midwife tomorrow."

"A midwife?"

"Yes S... Glennie says it is time." She felt lonely in this house even with the ruckus of giggly girls, instrumental music practice, racquetball coaching and dancing lessons. If it wasn't for Glennie's amiable ways she thought she might have gone stark crazy.

"Oh. I see."

"Mr Ha... Jensen... I was wondering if I could come in and see you before I retire? I do get weary, and you know I retire early... but sometimes I would like to tell you about your house... or hear about your day. Just for a few minutes Sir... that is all."

"We could have supper together... perhaps."

Her eyes lit up. "Oh, that is a very good idea. Yes. I would like that."

"Well, tonight then... after dinner... here in the library."

Elizabeth went straight to find Glennie. Elizabeth opened her book. "Glennie I have made a housekeeping plan, but it seems I may be missing things. I know that you have been doing these things for a very long time, but could you check what I have missed?"

"Well, I ain't one for reading much... but if you tell me what you've got, I can say what I think."

"Oh, Glennie, thank you!"

She read out the items and every so often Glennie would interject. Elizabeth took out her writing set and added to the lists in her book. When they were done, Elizabeth snapped her book closed. "Now I have another request. I want you to show me how to cook a sweet. Something Mr Jensen likes."

"Mr Jensen generally doesn't like sweets."

"Well, it doesn't matter what exactly... anything. Just something to have with tea... for supper. What could I do?"

Glennie offered a couple of options. None of them seemed very appetizing but Elizabeth settled on plain oatmeal biscuits, based on the ingredients in the pantry. She was so excited, as she was shown how to bank the fire the oven, and measure, and mix and spoon and flatten. "Oh, this is more wonderful than I ever imagined. Thank you, Glennie. Thank you," she enthused as she slid the tray into the oven.

"You have a knack for this Ma'am. I was thinking that your idea of cooking lessons was just a thing to say. I'm hoping you are not intending to put me out of a job?"

"Oh no, Glennie! Hush. What would we ever do without you? It has taken me longer than I thought to get used to the housekeeping. I get so tired. It is such a big house."

"That it is Ma'am. Mrs Harker came from a well-to-do family... not that Mr Harker couldn't hold his own in that department... but he just doted on her. The house belonged to her family originally. It caused quite a ruckus that she was bequeathed the estate when her Uncle passed on, being a woman and all. But the other cousin was abroad, and they didn't want it left vacant. He wasn't willing to lease it at all... and so it all became quite the point of society talk for a while. In the end, he died overseas, and I've always said it was fitting that a family with children live in a big house like this. But now they are saying that because it went to the niece, there is a curse on this place and that is why sadness visits. I never did take much stock in superstitions, but I got to say it is all looking pretty convincing now…"

"Really? Jensen says he is not superstitious at all. Don't you think that could change with a baby? Jensen says that a baby is happy news. I'm sure there could be smiles again."

"We'll see ma'am. We'll see. I am liking that Mr Jensen is talking more though. Didn't hear nor see him after the accident for nigh three months. Just retracted like a snail. It was just about on the threat of his life that he went to Mrs Grissom's ball."

"Well, Mrs Grissom must have some sway to get him there."

"Huh. No accounting for some things I guess."

After the girls had said their goodnights, Elizabeth went into the kitchen and as she arranged her biscuits on the plate, she felt a flutter of anticipation. She walked carefully into the library holding the tea tray. Jensen looked up and put down his book. He cleared a space on the low table near his chair. Elizabeth tried not to sound excited, but she could hardly contain herself. "Glennie gave me a cooking lesson. This is the first thing that I have ever baked! Glennie did supervise me very closely so I am sure that they will be edible."

"Oh..." He felt less than enthusiastic. Why did he ever suggest this rendezvous? It was not wise. It seemed that she was getting used to him, but he had not been able to quite get used to her.

"You must try one," Elizabeth said leaning over

the tray and pouring his cup of tea. He looked at her and noticed for the first time the swelling of her maternal bump, no longer concealed so well under layers of fabric.

He swallowed hard and grabbed at his tea-cup. He never expected to react like this. He gulped quickly to cover his shock, and gagged as he scalded his palate. "Oh! That is hot! Glennie doesn't come so promptly with the supper-tray perhaps."

"Oh, Jensen! I am so sorry! Are you okay? Here, have a drink of water." She passed a glass and he quickly guzzled a mouthful.

He took a deep breath and shook his head. How could supper become complicated? It was absurd. "Okay. Okay. That is better. So, these are the proceeds from your first batch of cooking?" he asked sceptically as he added a dash of cold water to his tea. Elizabeth picked up the plate and shoved it under his nose. He had little option but to choose a biscuit. He tentatively took a bite and then raised his brow. "Oh. These are good. Perhaps you are a natural."

Elizabeth glowed, bobbed her appreciation and then shook herself. "Well thank you, Jensen. Although I am never truly sure whether you are acting or not."

"Elizabeth, let me assure you that when we are alone, I have always endeavoured not to pretend. I want us to at least be candid friends."

"Can I be candid Jensen?"

"Hmm?"

"Why do you put yourself through this? You are so sad with Mrs Harker gone… and you don't need a housekeeper, Sir. You really don't. Glennie has always had things under control. Wouldn't it have been easier just not to bother? It seems that having me here just makes you miss her more. And I am so sorry that is so. I want to make you happy, but Susanna and Eunice are so troubled. Which part about this plan has been a good idea?"

He sipped his tea again. Another question. How was it possible that her questions unnerved him so? "You. You Elizabeth: you are the good idea." He took another bite just to find the silence in his head. That hollow vacant silence. "You and your baby are the good idea. I believe that. I really do."

"But Sir… how will you ever get used to me being here when you miss her so much?"

He regulated his breathing and closed his eyes while he took another drink. Her words echoed his own haunted thoughts. "You had some ideas on how to get used to me, and they seemed to have been effective to some degree. Perhaps these will help me?"

"Oh, really? Like what?"

"Like this… listening to you… talk."

"Do I talk too much?"

"No…" How was it that a man who enjoyed quietness attracted women so insistent on filling his silence? "But perhaps it could help me get used to having you here."

Elizabeth brought in the tray and set it on the table. Jensen was standing at the bookshelf replacing an armful of volumes. When he had unhurriedly finished his organising, he turned and realised that Elizabeth had been sitting for a while. He really did get lost in this literary world that was his refuge. He rebuked himself and promised to make more of an effort. He came over, rubbing his hand through his hair.

"What are you looking at?"

"It is your family Bible. I wondered if there were any family traditions that you had in naming your children."

"Hmm? Names? For the baby?"

"Oh, it is alright if there isn't. I thought that might be nice, but it is not necessary…"

"No. No. You are right. It is something to consider. Umm…" He felt a little lost. He came over and sat down beside her.

This man… this unusual man had a presence about him he seemed completely unaware of. She noticed him sitting there beside her and sat very still. He awkwardly pointed to the family tree. "My mother's name is Susanna… which we have used. Georgina's mother's name was Eunice… which we have used. My grandmother's name was…"

Elizabeth quickly cut in. "If the baby is a girl could we call her Georgina? I know that is not usual, but she was so special to you… and I don't particularly want to call the baby Edwina… if that is the tradition."

He looked at her with a strange sense of marvel. They sat there, side by side and she stared at the family tree until it turned sort of blurry in her vision. The date of Georgina's death was penned in, but nothing else. By its very absence, it was another confirmation that this was not a real marriage. Not a marriage to acknowledge. Not one to write in a family bible.

"And if it is a boy?"

"Oh. I like Liam Benjamin Jensen. I see your grandfather's name was William, and Liam is a strong name… just the end part of William. And your mother's father was Benjamin."

"You seem to have thought about this…"

She blushed. She had. Oh yes, she had. But she didn't want him to know. She had riffled through the family linage looking for the justification of her choice. It was not as hard as she had thought it might be. She held her breath to see if he might notice. But not today; he was not looking for the underneath today.

He shrugged. "Seems as reasonable as any choice." He smiled and stood up and resumed his seat opposite her. "Let's hope it is a girl."

"Yes, Sir. I'm sure it is… if it would make you happy." If it was a girl, no one would ever suspect that she had chosen to name her son after William Benjamin Madsen: her Bill. He might have rejected her, but he had also shown her what it was like to be the centre of someone's love and attention, for however short that moment was. Her baby was conceived in that moment... not the moment of rejection. She quietly and slowly let out her breath and put down the bible to pour the tea. It was nigh cold, but Jensen didn't notice.

Jensen came in early from work and found Elizabeth sitting on the lounge in his library. The bible was open, and she sat like stone. She jolted as she quickly closed the book and picked up her duster. She turned her face away, wet with tears. "Elizabeth, get some tea will you?"

"Yes, Sir."

She disappeared and dried her face on her apron as she went to the kitchen. She apologised to Glennie as she wiped the tray with a cloth.

Glennie raised her brow. "He wants tea now?"

She nodded and arranged the linen tray liner.

"Well, I never..."

"What?" Elizabeth positioned the cup and saucer.

"I reckon he's taken a fancy to you ..."

"Oh no, I don't think so. It is just tea..."

Elizabeth gasped and paled as she realised she had just disclosed their sacred secret. They were supposed to be husband and wife ...already married... already in love... already fancied.

Glennie winked as Joe came in the back door and dumped a sack of flour on the floor in a puff of powder. "Master Jensen never did fancy his tea as much as when you bring it to him. Take him his tray with another of your biscuits," Glennie said with typical firmness. She handed Elizabeth the little pot of tea in a cosy.

She looked hopeful, and Glennie nodded encouragingly. "You're his wife ain't you?" Elizabeth blushed and picked up the tray. Glennie immediately became intensely focused on mixing the batch of pastry on the floured bench, her hands sticky with the dough.

As Elizabeth left, Joe raised his brow at his wife and cautiously cleared his throat. "You ain't meddling where you're not needed now are ya?" said Joe severely.

Glennie floured her hands, grabbed a bottle and started rolling the pastry for their dinner pies without a pause. "Never seen two people so lonely living side by side. They just need eyes to see what is right in front of them."

Elizabeth put down the tray on the small table beside Jensen's chair. He said nothing but poured the tea, a ritual he liked to attend to himself when they were alone. "Do you want a cup?"

"Oh. I didn't set two cups."

"You can go and get one."

"Oh no… I won't bother thankyou…"

"Well remember next time, in case you feel like it. Have a biscuit."

She picked up a biscuit from the plate and nibbled around the edges. She wondered what it would be like to add fruit to this recipe. It was a random, unconscious thought, a distraction from the awkwardness of this interview.

"You were reading when I came in. Anything in particular?"

"I was tired and taking a break," she said apologetically.

"This is not another form of a sweat-shop. You are allowed to rest."

She was relieved he wasn't irritated with her. "I was actually looking at a picture. I was very moved by it."

"A picture?"

She felt her defences rise. Of course, he would think she was silly to look at pictures. "The words tell the story one way; this artist tells it another way." She leant over and tentatively turned to the illustration plate.

"Oh?" He came and looked over her shoulder. "I usually only like the word version… but I would like to see what you notice."

"I wondered what it might be like to be there. See how she is holding his feet so tightly? She loves him so much. Her tears show the depth of her feeling. And he hasn't rejected her... or ignored her. In fact, he is showing the others what she is doing even though they look very angry." Tears brimmed to the surface. Did he get it? Did Jensen really understand? "This could be me. This *is* me! This is my story."

"Your tears... are they tears of love too? Or tears of sadness?"

"A bit of both. I love him. Jesus notices me... but the others don't. I am sad I am not noticed by those who matter to me." *You matter to me... but you don't see me. You...* she didn't say it out loud, but she was surprised how that thought bubbled to the surface so quickly... so frankly. She wanted to be seen by him. Again. There were glimpses at the Beachside when he seemed to look right into her soul? And then he would retract, and she was invisible again. She wanted him to notice her tears... she wanted him to accept her love, however young and unformed it may be. Unformed like the baby growing within her: moving and developing, taking on shape and personality... but still unseen and unknown. She felt the baby move, and something deep within her was touched by the profound parallel. More tears fell.

Jensen reached out with his kerchief and gently dabbed her tears. "Perhaps there is a bit of both of us in this story," he said quietly. "Perhaps I hold his feet too."

Elizabeth gasped. "You? But you have not sinned... not like that."

"Oh, Elizabeth... perhaps my adultery is being married to you... and still loving another to your neglect. I need to find a way to let go. Perhaps holding the feet of Jesus is a way to start..."

10.

Jensen was ushered into the boardroom: the dark wood panelling, reflected in the dark surly faces around the table. Each man wore a suit, a cravat and a scowl as they sat in the deep leather-padded chairs heavily studded with raised upholstery-pins. Jensen was a little bemused as to why this distinguished group was assembled without discussion or notification. He was a founding partner of the firm. These men were his colleagues at the very least; some of them long term friends. Some even qualified as family. He pulled out his chair and supposed that, given his grief and extended leave, they were going to take this opportunity to bring him up to speed. He'd been back for a few weeks at varying levels of attentiveness, but now he felt he was ready to resume his load. He needed the distraction.

"So, gentlemen. It has been a while. I want to thank you for your patience. Our family is getting through this very difficult time. I've appreciated the graduated return, but I'm ready to work with a full client load again. Where do we start?"

The chairman cleared his throat. "Jensen. We are here to discuss one particular matter."

He nodded sagely... and felt no unease. "Of course. Whatever needs to be done."

"We have a specific concern that we must

address." There was a murmuring of consensus around the table while he paused. "We heard that you were recently married."

Jensen adjusted his glasses and felt the strangest twinge in his stomach. "You know I was. Why? Is this a concern?"

"Well, we don't understand why this news came to us third hand. You have not provided us with details. No one was invited."

"I guess because whom I marry is a private matter."

"On this, we disagree. Our lives are very much open to public scrutiny."

For a moment Jensen swallowed. Had Elizabeth spoken about the circumstances of their betrothal? Had her mother been less than discreet? He had been confident Edwina would not bear the shame of this becoming public. Perhaps she had spoken to Mrs Grissom, or let it slip in a moment of inebriated drama. He wished he had been clearer: blatantly explicit regarding his expectations. This was strictly a family matter. It had to be. Always. "I still don't understand why this is a concern."

Grissom spoke up. "It is not even six months since our beloved Georgina was suddenly taken from us."

"You may remember that it was you and Mrs Grissom who insisted that I socialize. You hosted a ball; even in the face of such recent devastation."

"You were supposed to get out and meet people: not elope! Whoever thought you would up and abscond with the first skirt who threw herself at your fortune! I would never have believed it of you, Harker. The girl's family was distraught thinking she had been abducted. It is unashamedly disrespectful of our family and theirs. Honour is the founding basis of this firm and it has been flagrantly disregarded."

Another spoke up. "We hear your wife is ridiculously young. You off having a honeymoon while Georgina's family is still in mourning decries common decency."

In spite of the table of frowns that confronted him, Jensen breathed a little easier. They did not know. If they had that information they would have led with it. He put on his acting face and soberly looked around the table. "Is not grief comforted in the arms of another?"

"We heard she is handsome. A wisp of a thing…"

Oh, they had this all so very wrong… and their error was his safety. He nodded. "Oh yes, she is beautiful. Would my consolation seem more real to you if she was ugly?"

That was just too impertinent for what they were expecting. Someone sniggered, which was quickly smothered by an outcry of indignation. Grissom jumped to his feet. "This is outrageous! Georgina is, was, my brother's only daughter. Since his passing, you have been like a son to us. Yet while our family remains absolutely destroyed by the loss of Georgina, you carry on like a bull in must! I won't stand for it! I won't!"

Jensen raised his brow just a bit and couldn't hide just the slightest twinge of a smile. What he intended as an insult, came out sounding like they were in awe of his virile reputation. If only they knew the reality of it. But they didn't. If they had this picture in mind anything less would be barely conceivable. He cleared his throat and took a drink from the array of glasses on the tray in the centre of the table. "What is it that you want from me? Should I take more time?"

Grissom was on a roll. "Well, that is just putting up the rails after the horse has bolted. There is no retrieving this mess in my mind. I call for your resignation!"

Jensen gagged and froze. "Resign? That is ludicrous!" There was a murmuring of agreement and suddenly Jensen understood he was facing the full force of mutiny. "Gentlemen! You can't be serious? I have invested into this firm from its founding moments. I have given over and over, consistently for fifteen years. I have brought in profitable clients. You have no grounds to demand this just because I re-marry. Which I reiterate is a personal matter. I assure you it was attended to with the utmost sense of decorum and discretion given our family tragedy. Why else would I go to such lengths to keep it private? It is completely legal. There was no immorality." Okay. He admitted that last blow was aiming low because he knew as a fact there were men around the table whose moral compasses were not exemplary. How dare they throw rocks?

One man stood up, red in the face, his waistcoat bulging. "Decorum? I disagree. Even if you did have an affair, and it was kept hidden, who would be disturbed? It happens. But instead, you choose a course of action that would eventually be open for everyone to scrutinise! And she is already pregnant! That can only be described as debauchery! You obviously have no regard for the appearances of principled conduct. If it was merely us, we could look the other way, but our clients are not always as magnanimous as ourselves. You have carried the firm's most lucrative accounts; and this directly damages the trust from our clientele. This is about what is best for the firm. It always is. That will always be our first priority."

He almost laughed. They made it sound as if business in general, and their business in particular, held all the veneration of the hallowed halls of the papacy. "Gentlemen, I am not going to resign."

"We demand it!" There were enthusiastic interjections around the table. Jensen could almost hear the rabble cry "Crucify!" This was beyond belief.

He stood to his feet. "I am not going to sit here and have my wife and my family smeared with such vulgar innuendo! I will speak to my solicitor and get some legal advice. I am a founding partner. I have always invested with integrity. This is unacceptable to me on every level." He stood up and walked out, and the uproar that he left behind faded as he closed the door to the office and walked down the stairwell.

Jensen stepped off the running board of the buggy at the botanical gardens and paid the taxi-driver. He walked along the shaded path, mottled with sunlight until he found a bench to sit on. He put his head in his hands. Was he so off-centre? Was his compass so morally depraved that he just couldn't see it? Was he so blind? Would Georgina judge him as severely as those faces around the table? 'Bull in must'… really? He shook his head. Had they expected rage? Would they be surprised by the crazed indignation that boiled in his chest? He clenched his fist in his fury and silently swore at the sky.

11.

Elizabeth was dusting the banister rail and wiping the wood with an oiled rag as she walked down the stairs, humming. She looked up to see Jensen staring at her. She smiled uncertainly. "Good afternoon. You are home early today."

"Yes. I wondered if you could rustle up a pot of tea and bring it to me in the library?"

"Certainly! I will be there very shortly."

She quickly piled the tray with a plate of biscuits and freshly brewed tea. Two cups. She liked it when she was summoned to his library. She felt flattered that he wanted to sit with her.

"I have a splitting headache," he said without ceremony as she put down the tray. He rubbed his forehead and leaned back in the lounge. It was an open disclosure, given without hesitation. Elizabeth wished she felt comfortable enough to rub his temples like her Maudy used to do in the nursery when she was very little. Maudy would gently massage away her distress when she had cried so hard that her head complained. But Elizabeth didn't dare make such a gesture; she didn't want to add embarrassment to his discomfort, and she didn't want to be told to go away.

Eventually, he sat up and she quickly came over to pour his tea. "Something happened today," he offered.

"Oh?" She felt herself go a little stiff. She sat down opposite him and hung on tightly to the arm of the chair.

"I was called into a meeting at work. I expected it to be a polite sort of affair where they would give me reassurances of their support while I settle back in." He shook his head and put down his cup.

Elizabeth stared at him. His face contorted in all sorts of ways as he struggled to articulate what had transpired.

"I... Well. I guess you have gathered it wasn't that. They want me to resign."

"What?" She didn't understand.

"Resign. Leave the firm. They want me to go."

"Sir, don't you own it? You said that you owned it... or part of it. How can they ask you to leave?"

"Exactly! Exactly."

"Sir, did they give a reason?"

"Yes, they did."

She sat there silently... waiting for the verdict. Perhaps when he was at work he was very different to the man that she so unwaveringly wanted to believe him to be.

"I don't know what I should tell you. I don't want to upset you."

"Oh." Panic glowed in her chest. Too late for that. Perhaps they had caught him doing something unethical, or incompetent, or criminal. "Please tell me the rest."

"I should have said nothing."

"Perhaps. But now you have started I would hear the worst of it. Are you going to be arrested?"

"What? Arrested? No!" He stared at her in shock. "Okay: I guess I do have to finish." He took a breath. In a way, her projection helped add perspective. "They feel that I did not wait long enough in my bereavement before I remarried."

"So, it is not about your work? You haven't done anything wrong?"

"They think this is very wrong."

"That you married me?"

"Married anyone. This is not about you Elizabeth. Their concern is that I have not respected Georgina or her family."

"That is ridiculous Sir! You love her so much."

"Why is it that you seem to be the only one to talk any sense? I cannot fathom where they get their ideas."

"But Jensen this is about me. You only married quickly because of my situation. You must explain that to them."

"No, I must not!"

"But you must let them know that it was your kindness and charity that precipitated our early marriage."

"No! Never! Elizabeth, please hear me. No one, I reiterate: '*no one*' must ever know that this baby is anything other than our honeymoon child. This is absolutely critical. My daughters' future lives and reputations depend on it. If you will not do it for yourself, you must, absolutely must, do it out of gratitude on what we agreed. Please! I cannot emphasise enough how important this is." He looked at her gravely. "Promise me."

Her eyes filled with tears. She came around and knelt beside the lounge. "This is so unfair. They have branded you unfeeling, and yet you suffer every moment of every day from your loss. They think you are cold and yet you have put aside your own preferences of being alone in your grief to make a place for me and our baby. They have branded you a monster, and yet you are the gentlest, most respectful, caring man I have ever met. Please, Jensen. You must vindicate yourself! You must. They should not push you out for something you did not do. They would reconsider if they knew."

"They would not. They have made up their minds."

"But surely..."

"Elizabeth. I have worked with them for fifteen years. I know how they think. It is the appearance of things that win."

She let out a sob and clutched his knee. "I have not only broken your heart... I have destroyed your vocation. Is there anything that I touch that doesn't shatter?"

He felt himself melt at the pressure of her hand.

He reached down and lifted her to the seat beside him on the lounge. "Oh Elizabeth, you have not broken my heart... you are helping to mend it. This is not your fault." He drew her in for an embrace and as he held her and felt her body beside him, warmth and comfort infused him. A flutter of a movement, barely perceivable, moved in her belly against his. Here was a tangible reason to fight: to protect his family... this family. Was consolation really within reach, not just as an ignorant accusation, or a theory?

She sat up and pulled away. "You could send me away," she said with determination.

"No, I could not. That is senseless. You are my wife."

"Well, what if I left? What if I run away? Then you would be free of me."

"I would find you and bring you home. How would that solve anything? Not only will I have committed the crime of marrying prematurely, but I would also have added to that the bad reputation of not looking after my wife appropriately. That is nonsense thinking."

"What if I explained it to them? If you were not speaking for yourself they would see the kind of moral man you are."

"Elizabeth! Stop it now! They do not want to see. I cannot change that. Neither can you. Promise me!"

She stood up startled at his tone and burst into

tears again. "But what if they don't change their mind? What if they make you go?"

"Then we will work it out. I have spoken to a solicitor briefly. I have a longer appointment on Monday. I am going to fight this the whole way." And he went over to her and held her again. He kissed her forehead, and she flung her arms around him and cried into his shoulder.

"I promise... but only because you ask it of me. This is not right," she sobbed.

12.

One morning Jensen ushered a plain-looking young woman into the room where Elizabeth was sitting, staring at the housekeeping book in her lap. She was adding some notes to the 'Nursery' page.

"Elizabeth? This is Marjorie. She is the daughter of Glennie's cousin."

She smiled. "Hello, Marjorie. It's always nice to meet Glennie's family. It's lovely that you have the opportunity to visit her." She wondered at the introduction. For some reason, it felt a bit like she was being presented as the "Lady of the House".

Jensen cleared his throat. "Actually, she is not visiting. As your time is getting closer the priority is for you to take care of yourself. She will do whatever you require of her. Household chores. Nursery duties after the baby is born. Anything you might need."

"Oh." She glanced at her book and said, "Well, Marjory there's a lot of laundry needed to set up the nursery. You could start there."

Jensen nodded and sent Marjory on her way. Elizabeth looked expectantly at him as he stood there, but evidently, he had nothing further to say except, "I trust Marjory being here will be helpful. Is everything else going well?"

"I believe so…"

"Oh. Okay then." He cleared his throat again

and she heard the Library door close soon after he left the room.

Elizabeth sighed and put down the book. She got up and went for a walk in the garden. After a while she sat on the garden chairs, her body heavy and uncomfortable. So, he didn't realise. Or if he did, he had no intention of marking it in any way. She tried not to be disappointed. After all, it probably was to be expected.

Still, it was weird for her, sitting here, on this day. This time last year she was in a flurry preparing to host Farthing's social calendar event of the year under the militant supervision of her mother. Sixteen! She was vivacious, carefree, beautiful, and her dance card was full, sought after by many young men. That night Mother had informed her she had finally been able to convince Mr Madsen to start her working at the store. Mother had also quietly raised her brow and said it was appropriate she should get to know his son. That night was the first time she danced with Bill. She never understood, when it was obvious her mother desired the match, why three months later, they would flee town because of that very same thing.

How differently everything looked now! Technically, she was the lady of a large house. Technically she was the wife of an influential and wealthy man. Technically she had everything her baby would need. And yet, she also felt very alone. Who would have thought that her seventeenth birthday would look like this? Not her. Not in a million years.

Perhaps her mother was right. Perhaps she would miss all of those years of being the pampered daughter of Edwina Perkins. Something occurred to her then: the daughter of Edwina. It was never about her. She was only ever the daughter. And all those years she had lived in the secure delusion of believing it was about her, that her indulgence was about her affection. But no, it was not. Suddenly she realised that her father had in so many ways been the intermediary... and he had played a much larger role in her sheltered life than she ever gave him credit for. And then another thought occurred to her. Perhaps it would not have mattered too much how she grew up... whether by an unplanned pregnancy, or getting a job of her own choosing, or marrying someone else. At some point, if or when she chose her own path, the focus would shine off her mother and she would have suffered the same rejection with accusations of shame. Is this what growing up was all about? Was it making and accepting those choices with all their flaws and living your life anyway? Choosing to love it anyway.

There was one thing that Elizabeth decided she knew about herself. She was not afraid of trying. She would try, over and over, to be improved, to be better, to strive to do well with what was placed in her hand. But suddenly she decided that she didn't want to keep trying to please her unpleasable mother. Not anymore. There were other people in her life now. And suddenly her expectations were developing and moulding with a different awareness. And although she had rarely allowed herself to be someone she needed to please, she would try to include herself as one of the people she cared for. And she would start today. After all, didn't Jensen say she was to look after herself? She suspected what he really meant was she must look after the baby, but if she waited for Jensen to notice her, or her birthday... it was entirely possible that she could turn ninety and never celebrate another birthday ever. She wondered what she could do to mark her birthday when no one else was even aware of it? It was not that she expected anyone to notice her particularly. Of course not. But it was her birthday. So, even with all the tiredness and pain and stretching in her body... she decided to bake herself a cake. Not just any cake but bake her very first birthday cake. That would be a wonderful way to mark her birthday.

She stood up and stretched her shoulders and back. She felt the tightness of her pregnant body contracting as she moved. Yet she would not be shifted from completing her assignment. She went into the kitchen and found Glennie sorting through her pantry.

"Glennie... I have come to bake a cake. A birthday cake."

"Whose birthday is it?"

"Mine."

"Oh? When?"

"Today."

"Oh? Well, that seems to be as good as reason as any. What sort of cake do you want? Now I have some very good and faithful recipes... and there are many that I like. Are you partial to fruit cake, or a..."

"Apple cake I think..."

"Oh? That's a very unusual choice for a birthday cake... but it just so happens that my Aunt Dotty... on my mother's side... Marjorie's' grandmother actually... she has the most treasured recipe that was given to her by a very dear friend. Dotty's Apple cake is always a sought-after favourite at our family get-togethers."

"Oh yes! That sounds perfect."

"Well, I will get right to it now and whip it up for dessert."

"Oh no, Glennie. My birthday gift is that I bake it myself. I want you to teach me the recipe."

"Really my dear? Do you think you should be cooking at a time when you could lean over and your baby pop right out? You can't be cooking when you are so heavily pregnant."

"Why not? Who says that this is a rule? Jensen encourages me to challenge conventional wisdom. I want to do this."

"But what if he finds you here... steaming over an oven?"

"Then he may make allowances since it is my birthday."

"He's giving you allowances for your birthday?"

"Well no... but only because he doesn't realise."

"Perhaps you might remind him? He can be distractible."

"It really doesn't matter whether he realises it or not. My birthday party will be cooking a cake. Let's start now."

So, they creamed and folded and greased and lined and poured and peeled and sliced and sprinkled and baked. She laughed as she slid the pan into the oven and lifted her arms in the triumph of success. As she spun around, she saw Jensen staring at her from the doorway. Glennie put down the towel she was holding and mumbled something about needing to pull more carrots from the garden for dinner and started for the back door.

"Glennie! What is going on here?"

"Ahh... baking Sir. Baking a cake."

"Whatever for? Don't you think this is a little unreasonable to have Elizabeth in the kitchen cooking when she has been taken off other duties?"

Elizabeth stopped and turned slowly. "I'm sorry... taken off duties? No one has taken anything off me, Sir!"

"Of course, you have. Marjorie is here to alleviate your workload."

"You said she was here to help, not take over!"

"And since Glennie is our cook, she is to attend to..."

"You said Glennie could teach me to cook and

she is doing exactly what I have asked of her. She is not stepping outside anything that you have agreed to."

"Elizabeth. That is enough."

"No, I don't think it is enough! You agreed I could cook... and I wanted to cook. So, I am cooking!"

Jensen stared at her bewildered, almost like he was witnessing a possession. Whatever happened to the compliant, affable Elizabeth? His voice went very quiet. "I say this not to be disagreeable, but because I need you to look after yourself."

"Of course, you do. Because it would be so terribly inconvenient if something occurred to disrupt your reading time! I want to cook. So, I am cooking! I wasn't disturbing you, so what is disagreeable is that you are accusing Glennie of being neglectful. She has been nothing short of incredible. I have had the most wonderful time."

"Elizabeth..."

"Oh, stop using that tone on me! I am not your daughter. I am supposed to be your wife!" She flounced past him and out of the room, well at least as much as a fully pregnant body can flounce. She went outside and sat down at her refuge in the garden. It was a relief to have a private space to breathe... away from every prying eye. Breathe... just breath...

She took another deep breath and rubbed her lower back. She smiled as she thought about her cake. It was like an oasis in a dry and thirsty land. She was not going to give up cooking just when she had discovered it.

As she walked inside later, Glennie ushered her wordlessly into the Library. "Sir, as you requested… Mrs Harker is here." He sort-of flinched and stood up as the door closed.

Elizabeth felt the line of her mouth go hard. "A lot of good being 'Mrs' when I can't even…" Then she smelt the Apple Cake and looked around. There on the table was her Apple Cake, presented gloriously on a serving plate, positioned near the tea tray. "Oh look! It has turned out wonderfully! It looks so… well just like the one a saw in a bakery once, with the crystallised sugar sprinkled over the apple pieces. I was hoping it would be like that." She smiled broadly. "I made this!"

Jensen turned and stared at her face. "You did."

She giggled. "I trust I did not shame Aunt Dotty. I'm not sure either Glennie or Marjorie would approve if that was the case."

"I think she would be proud. Shall we try a piece for afternoon tea? We can share the rest at dinner with the girls. Glennie tells me today is a special day."

"Oh yes! You must critique it quite seriously. I want to do this better next time. Apple Cake is not as sweet as some other cakes, but there is the spice that gives it a perfect balance of flavour to accompany a cup of tea." She came over and picked up the knife and cut a slice with a shy smile. "I read that in a book. You have to tell me if you agree," she said quite eagerly as she handed it to him.

He sat down and nodded seriously as he took the plate and cake fork from her hand. She sat opposite him and stared at his face expectantly. He paused and looked at her. He went to say something and then drew his focus back to the plate in his hand. He slowly broke into the cake and noted how it had the right amount of crumble... not too dry. He smelt it with his eyes closed and commented on the blend of aromas, apple and cinnamon. He tasted it carefully and tried to think of something he could say that might be considered constructive, but nothing came to mind so he described what he did enjoy... the softness of the apple underneath and the crunch of the caramelised sugar on top. She poured his cup of tea and handed it to him with a look of complete satisfaction.

"I thought birthdays were about pampering the one celebrating the birthday... not having treats cooked for me," he observed as he sat back and drank his tea and finished the cake. "This is perfectly pleasant."

"Thank you, Jensen."

"You thank me?"

"Yes. For taking my cooking seriously. That was the best birthday gift. Better than anything."

"Does this mean I take this back?" He referred to the small wrapped gift on the tray next to the teapot.

"Oh… Well. I think I am ready for it now."

"Right then," and he picked it up and passed it to her. He held it for a moment in her hand. "Elizabeth, I am sorry for my tone. I am sorry that sometimes you feel I behave like a parent. I would like to think 'protective' maybe… but I… I apologise… not that I am protective of course, but that it feels… paternal. You are right. I am not your father; I am your husband. I am also sorry that I did not take notice that today was a special day for you. I trust I will do better next year."

She smiled a little. "I remember you once told me you found it worthwhile having your life a provoking combination of wilfulness and challenge. I think that you should have the most interesting life being married to me, Sir."

"I have no doubt."

"Well, it seems I am right after all."

"Right about what exactly… that you are wilful and challenging?"

She laughed. "Oh, I am not sure I could accurately judge that. I was thinking that you are a most unusual man. Most unusual. Thank you…" she said quietly.

"You are thanking me for being odd?"

"No. I am thanking you for marrying me…"

"You are welcome, Mrs Harker."

"Well, that still sounds strange." She turned her attention to her gift and unfolded the wrapping paper.

She opened a small jewellery box revealing a heart pendant on a chain. It matched the setting of her engagement ring... a centre diamond, encircled with emeralds and rubies. "Oh. Wow. Thank you."

"Happy birthday Elizabeth. It came as a set when I bought your ring. Now you have both."

"This is very generous Sir."

"Hmm... but not as generous as a serious appraisal of your cooking?"

"Do you think it strange that I value your attention, and your comments, as much as an expensive necklace?"

"Perhaps both are needed." He stood up and took the pendant from her hand. He stood behind her and fastened it at the nape of her neck. She shivered under his touch and he paused for just a moment before he fastened it. Then she quickly cut another piece of cake for them both to eat, a blush running up into her cheeks.

13.

Susanna stood defiantly beside the table. "Sit down please Susanna. There is something that I wish to say. I want us all to be aware of this."

"I am aware. I am completely aware that our lives have been ruined and it is all her fault. We were doing fine before she came along."

Elizabeth sat silently at the table. She wondered if it was possible to feel any more tired and awkward. And yet with every day that passed, she did. Susanna's tirade was predictable, if unfair. Just another onslaught. It felt like Susanna and the baby were in cahoots to make her life miserable. The baby was moving roughly, and she felt a pang shoot through her pelvis. It took her breath away and she slowly rubbed her belly. It seemed she ached all through.

Glennie had been adamant for months. "You are carrying all out in front. Never seen it be wrong. That is a boy to be sure. A big boy... tall like his dad." Elizabeth wondered if she really suspected who the baby's father was... or wasn't. With the loyalty of a legionnaire, Glennie never challenged the paternity of the child, just the timing of it. Why else would someone like Mr Harker marry quickly like this? Elizabeth could not resolve why it was important for Glennie to accurately predict the baby a boy because the only indication Jensen gave of his preferences came from naming a girl Georgina. Just now she wondered if the baby, girl, or boy, was playing tiggy-tag. She hoped it was not a sign of a raucous, hard-to-manage child to come.

"Susanna! If you cannot be quiet, you will not hear what it is I have to tell you."

"I don't want to hear it."

"Very well. You may leave. But do not complain when you do not understand what is going on."

She raised her eyebrows and folded her arms. It took the sting out of her defiance when her father made it permissible. "Fine. I'll stay," she snapped and sulkily sat down.

Jensen sat opposite her. He had wanted the setting for this conversation to be orderly and composed because what was coming would certainly be challenging. He set the preliminaries aside and dived right in: "I am selling the estate."

Susanna was on her feet again in a moment. "You can't. This was Mama's inheritance. Ours!"

"Mine actually. The property comes to me. I don't have to justify or explain my decision: I am choosing to let you know of my plans."

"This is outrageous!" She turned on Elizabeth, sitting white-faced and still. "You! You have poisoned him against us. You have just been after our money from the start."

"Susanna. Sit down. Now." Carrying authority

was something Jensen never found difficult, but sometimes Susanna's wilfulness challenged him in ways few other things did. "If you are concerned about your inheritance, then on that point I can reassure you. This one estate is chewing up money at a great rate. By the time you are at the age of majority, the upkeep and maintenance will be so enormous it will be virtually worthless. From there it will just put us into debt. But the property as it currently stands is very marketable. There are not many properties available that hold as much prestige as this. My choice is to keep one property or to invest more broadly. You have a head for figures, Susanna. You can see the sense. Keeping the estate to increase our debt to maintain it will only leave us with massive liabilities. Or we can use this money to diversity our holdings that will give us a return. Once the sale is finalised we will be able to secure a number of different properties around town. My goal is not to have just one property to split between all of you... but for each of you to have a couple of solid real estate investments each. This is the better course."

"You can't mean her."

"I remind you to address Elizabeth by name. And I assure you this does include my wife and our baby when she is born. I am keeping the Beachside Cottage, and we will move to a smaller less demanding property. My hope is that if you choose your investment now, there need be no squabbling when you have to work through bequest details."

Eunice stared at her father. "Are you sick Daddy? Are you dying? Is this why we are moving?" Tears filled her eyes.

"No! No, I am quite well. This is just to explain why such a big change is coming. It might seem like it is not an improvement moving to a smaller house; but overall, it secures our future much better."

When the girls left, Jensen leaned his elbows on the table and rubbed his brow. "Elizabeth, they are not going to change their mind. We have been back and forth for months, but they are digging in... mostly to save face and prove their control, I suspect. This is the main reason I am relinquishing the estate. It is too cumbersome on an income limited to investment returns."

"You lose everything?"

He smiled, a tired sort of look that sent waves of remorse through Elizabeth. "I have not lost anything. I still have my family."

"Oh Jensen... it hardly seems like enough." It totally astounded her how he never held the firm's decision against her. Jensen never belittled her lack of judgement in her relationship with Bill. He never judged her moral character as a fallen woman. As the time drew near for the baby to be born, these were the reflections that swirled around in her head. How was it then, that she still sometimes woke in the night, and would lie there wakeful, her heart pounding fresh from a dream about Bill? The imprint of his laughing eyes that she adored would suddenly turn and mock her. His affirmations about modern women that made her feel warm and strong would turn to outcries of not being good enough for the Madsen Empire. The kisses of affection that sent shivers of delight through her body would turn to exclamations of ridicule, her face burning with humiliation and degradation under the cries for a public stoning in Farthing's main street. And she would turn away from the regular breathing of Jensen sleeping beside her and allow the tears to fall silently. Part of her still loved Bill; part of her loathed him; and part of her wanted his handsome face to fill with remorse and beg her to return. She imagined the pleasure it would give her to back away with the scorn he had turned on her.

Jensen lifted his head from the table. "What I am working on now is how to retain my shares without my physical presence at the firm. It is still a good business."

"Oh!"

"It will be like a silent partnership," he explained patiently.

"Jensen?"

"The most infuriating thing is the exclusion articles that prohibit me from taking private clients... and I am working to have that loosened to allow some options to..."

"Jensen!"

He stopped and looked at her. He rarely heard Elizabeth talk with such emphasis. "Yes?"

"I think that the baby is coming."

He raised his brow as if he didn't quite believe her.

"My waters just broke."

He slowly tilted his head to look under the table, and there was an undeniable pool under her chair on the polished timber floor. "Okay. Well. I think I will get Glennie to come and see to this. Just stay here a moment. Don't move."

Suddenly Elizabeth felt very alone. Jensen was walking away. Fear gripped her heart and tears fell. Just then a contraction strangled her body and she let out a scream. Glennie came running in and she offered her a towel and helped her up. Jensen did not appear.

"Hush now girl... this is just the start. It isn't all roses, but as they say, this is the work of being a mother."

Elizabeth started to whimper. "I can't do this... I can't."

"You can and you must. You have a baby who is wanting to meet his mother... and it can't be put off. You just come with me... we will settle you in and the midwife will be here directly. Mr Jensen has gone to fetch her." She directed Elizabeth to the stairway and she barely made two steps before she shrieked and buckled under the intensity of another contraction. She had no idea they could start with such force. Didn't the book say labour began like the severe ache from a monthly flux?

"Come on now. We can get you upstairs. We've had the nursery room prepared for a long time. It is all ready for you and the little one. But we need to get there... it is not proper to be having a baby on the stairway."

Elizabeth made a gallant effort to move up a couple of steps, and then she stopped again, gripping the banister, groaning, and growling through the next contraction. "Now there, see: that is more like it," said Glennie with approval. "No screaming like a banshee. This is a mother doing the original mother's work. You seem quite natural at it really."

Elizabeth couldn't say for sure, what Glennie was even saying after that. All she heard was her prattling away... a bit like a kettle on the boil, as she edged her way... step by step towards the bedroom. She was barely aware of Eunice staring at her from her bedroom door, or of Susanna gaping openly with a satisfied smirk.

By the time the matronly midwife waddled in, Elizabeth was lying fitfully on the bed between contractions and then jolted awake as the next spasm hit her like a sledgehammer on an anvil.

It didn't take long for the midwife to appear bored. She sat in the easy chair and sipped a cup of tea. When Glennie fussed and clucked, she just raised her eyes above her rimless glasses and said, "Oh hush now. The baby is fine. That is a big baby, so you girl, have a lot more work to do for a while yet. Work like you've never done before. They don't call it labour for nothing. This will remind you that your pampered life of gallivanting around is now over." And Elizabeth just let out an unholy howl and screamed in agony.

Jensen heard that howl and jolted to his feet. He poured himself another drink... and another as the next cry slid down the banister into the library. Eventually, he just brought the canister over to the lounge and after a few more wails he didn't even bother with his glass.

He was roused by Glennie shaking his shoulder; then jolted awake as she impatiently flushed his face with a glass of water. "Mr Harker! Mr Harker! Jensen Sir! You are a father again. The babies have arrived. And they are fine-looking lads Sir! You have boys: twin boys!"

He was vaguely aware that his reading lamp flickered low on the table. "Elizabeth?"

Glennie nodded. "She did fine Sir. She did fine."

And he sighed with relief and leant back on the lounge, sliding into an unconscious stupor.

14.

Jensen woke to a blacksmith pounding at his temples. He struggled up and poured a glass of water and then pulled himself to the kitchen to find Glennie so she could prescribe something for his headache. He couldn't find her. All he remembered was the shock of that strangling fear that he would lose his wife... again. And then the avalanche of relief that he felt from Glennie's rough reassurance was beyond his comprehension. And the child? He wasn't sure he had heard correctly, but there was a nagging idea of not one baby, but two. He staggered up the stairs and the girls appeared at the top landing scandalized that no breakfast had been prepared.

Jensen stared at them, his face scruffy, and his eyes bloodshot. "Today you have the privilege of helping yourself. Have you seen the baby?"

They shook their head. The idea of a baby softened their antagonism towards Elizabeth with curiosity... just the slightest bit.

"Let me check..." He tapped at the door, and Glennie was there holding a bundle while Elizabeth sat in bed feeding the other with the midwife helping with great patience.

The midwife stood up and came over and whispered to him. "Mr Harker, you have twin boys! Fine little urchins they are Sir. Strong as can be. They are little Sir, as you would expect. And early... as you would expect. But I am confident they will be okay... they are breathing fine for being so early: strong little fighters these two. We may be feeding with droppers for a while. Your wife is doing well. Twins explain a lot. I've been doing this for many years, but these are my first twins. Many midwives don't ever get to deliver twins. They were just thirty-four minutes apart. I'm sorry Sir for my assumptions." It was a full confession.

He felt his tension unravel just a bit. "Thank you for your expertise, Sister. Would you mind... ... well, you know... if there are any doubts... clarifying, you know, about the dates?"

"Of course Sir. A brave effort for a first. Twins are a difficult thing... and she never missed a beat."

Sure. Elizabeth had gone from being a brazen tart to a war-hero in the space of thirty-four minutes. Thank God. He went to approach the bed, but the midwife steered him away deftly. He stared at Elizabeth over the midwife's shoulder, sitting in bed struggling with the mechanics of feeding, and she glanced up with a pained look in her eyes. Glennie came over and offered him to hold his oldest son. Jensen held him, tiny and crinkled... and he snorted and sneezed and cried a teeny weak cry. "Can I show the girls?"

"Oh, you can't take him out into the draughty corridor. Maybe stand by the door... just quickly..."

So, Eunice and Susanna were fleetingly given a peek through a gap in the door… a scrunched up little face, swimming in wraps.

Elizabeth sat in the chair, numb from exhaustion. The boys had finally settled. She hardly noticed who came and went, or even when Jensen came in and hovered over their cribs.

He sat down beside her and patted her arm encouragingly.

"You have done a fine job Elizabeth. The midwife says the boys are very strong even though they are small."

"Jensen? You never said, but I wanted to ask: are you disappointed that the baby wasn't a girl?"

"Disappointed? Not at all. I think the Divine has had mercy on me to restore the balance of the sexes to the Harker household." He grinned.

"Yes. That must be it: balance." She leant back on the cushions in the armchair and offered a tired smile. A weight lifted from her shoulders. He wasn't dissatisfied.

"The boys are making their mark just by being here."

That was true. How could two little people dominate a household with such tyranny? She felt terrible. Would life ever resume a steady rhythm? It seemed an impossible ambition just now. She thought that perhaps she should have felt relieved to have Marjorie's help, but in a way, the need to supervise someone seemed unnecessarily taxing, another demand on her depleted resources. But she had no choice, and no physical energy to do anything different.

Whatever delusional romantic ideal she had held about mothering being a routine of alternately caressing baby cheeks and rocking swaddling bundles of gurgling joy, was now smothered in the reality of laundry, nappies, soothing nerve-stretching crying, breastfeeding, exhaustion and pain. It was the pain that shocked her most. Her nipples were bleeding and her breasts felt like the Rock of Gibraltar. She couldn't really recall where the Rock of Gibraltar was, but one of her mother's travelled visitors had talked about it, and she remember looking it up in an atlas at school. To her, it sounded like a suitable metaphor for anything large and obnoxious. The cabbage poultices applied by the midwife seemed to do little to alleviate her pain. Her breasts felt so hot she was sure they would explode. Perhaps the Volcano Vesuvius in one of Jensen's history books was a more suitable picture. Elizabeth felt like she was being lowered into a bottomless pit called motherhood from which she would never escape. Was this why her mother was like she was? Is this why she fought and clawed and screamed her way out?

Even after three weeks the nursing sister was still

frowning and shaking her head when she came and pinched their little thighs. And every time Jensen came into the nursery, she felt so anxious. She didn't want to fail him. She couldn't. Not now. She had thought the delivery would be the worst of it, but it wasn't in the least. It was difficult and agonising, but it was over. This, on the other hand, seemed like it would go on forever and ever. She passed the baby to Glennie and went to stand up. She wavered. "I think I'm going to be sick…" she said weakly. She turned to Jensen and saw his face go white. That is all she remembered.

Jensen was sitting by her bed, silently holding her hand. His chin was rough and unshaven, and his hair unruly. Her eyelids flicked as she struggled to open her eyes. She started up with the anxious thought, "The babies! I think I dozed off. The babies! Are they okay?"

Jensen was alert in a moment. "Yes. Yes. They are fine. We have been looking after them. They are okay."

She took a drink of water from his hand and leant back against the pillows. "How long did I sleep? Did they miss a feed?"

"Ahh… Elizabeth? We had to get a wet-nurse. The boys are doing fine."

"A nurse? No! I don't want that. I am their

mother. I only just napped. I can go to them now…."

"You have been sick for days. You have been very unwell."

"I am awake now. I must feed them."

"Sister thinks that they will need the nurse until they are weaned."

"But that is not right. No one does that anymore. I should be able to feed them myself."

"People use nurses all the time. Some for no other reason than it is fashionable. It doesn't matter how the boys are fed as long as they are doing well. And more importantly… you will be able to make a full recovery."

She closed her eyes and felt the weight of the bed-clothes pinning her down. She tried to sit up. "No. I insist… I need to…" She went to get up, but she had already dozed off before she could move the covers away.

The next time she woke Jensen was sitting by the bed, shaved and hair combed. He was holding one of the boys deep in conversation gently rocking him in his lap. She lay there listening to his deep voice talk about the importance of combining quality workmanship with inventive design to create something lasting, and the baby looked at him wide-eyed tracing the movement of his mouth with his gaze. She smiled as she watched them; the sense of family washing over her, soothing her, like the waves on the sand at the Beachside Cottage. A tear escaped her eye and she let it roll down to the pillow unchecked.

Jensen looked up and stopped talking as his gaze connected with hers. "Well look, my little man, the beautiful Princess Briar-Rose has awoken from her enchanted sleep. Were you her prince who had the power to raise her? Here: talk to your mother and I will go and see if your brother has finished fussing. That one is always hungry." He placed Liam beside her in her arms and she held him humming quietly as she looked at his face. He seemed to have changed, his little cheeks chubbing out. Had she really been unwell for so long? Jensen came in with Ben, holding him as he squirmed and wriggled. "See, they are doing well. But they miss their mother. It is good that you are awake. Glennie says there is none who can settle this one like you."

She smiled again; a tired thin smile lined with exhaustion. And something very strange occurred to her. Even in sickness, life can be good when surrounded by good people. That's what she had. Good people. Good family. "You are a wonderful father, Jensen. These boys are lucky."

"Perhaps luck is shining her fickle face on me finally. What is good, is to see you awake. I wasn't sure I could do that again…"

"Do what?"

"Lose you too. I pleaded with The Almighty to spare me that. I know He has heard and answered my prayer."

She stared at his face, transparent with the agony of fear, and she realised something she had not realised before. He was no longer playing a role. This was the life he had chosen. He had chosen her.

She nodded. "I am awake now."

15.

By the time Elizabeth was back on her feet, resuming control over the housekeeping with the less than enthusiastic help of Marjorie and Hilary, the wet-nurse, the house move was well and truly on the agenda. One afternoon, Jensen took her on an outing to have a tour of the new house. When they pulled up outside Elizabeth stood at the gate speechless. Jensen looked at her apologetically. "I know that this is disappointing compared to the estate, but we can make it a very suitable home for us."

She looked confused. "You are embarrassed by this house?"

"I have logical reasons for this choice. There are spacious grounds for the boys as they grow. Plenty of rooms. They have good stables. It is a sound investment in a good area. I know the girls think it is somewhat inadequate, especially when our family has effectively doubled since you have come. By that rationale, they think it means we should be going bigger, not smaller."

Elizabeth walked up the front stairs of the rambling house with full verandahs and bay windows. She was quietly amazed. "I think this is beautiful."

"Really?" He was surprised by her acquiescence. He had been bracing himself for the rational arguments that had been the ongoing dialogue with

Susanna.

She wandered through the rooms with an appreciative eye. The estate house was too cavernous and cold to be homely. "The Estate was your home with Georgina. This feels like our home. It is even bigger than the house I grew up in Farthing, and out there it was considered one of the finer homes in the community. This is perfect." She reached up and kissed his cheek. "I love it."

Jensen was thoughtful on his way back home. Even now he could feel her breath on his face. Had he expected Elizabeth to behave like another headstrong teenage daughter? Was he again treating her more like a wilful child rather than his wife? Yet here she had shown quiet, sensible maturity. He really admired sensible.

There were a number of things that required downsizing. Elizabeth was given the list of items needed to furnish their new home, and it was her job to choose what to keep. The large carriage was downgraded to a smaller buggy. The fourteen seat dining suite was exchanged for a regular table, seating eight. Some special furniture pieces were set-aside for Susanna and Eunice. Everything else that wasn't brought with them was sold as part of the estate.

Sacrificing the Library was Jensen's greatest challenge. The new house only had a routine size study. So, after the carpenter fitted the room with floor-to-ceiling bookshelves, he had to choose which of his very favourite books would go with him. He spent a great deal of time sorting through his Library shelves boxing up books to send to a community library.

Elizabeth came into the library on their last night at the estate. She walked around boxes and crates of books. "Is it difficult to let these go? You have many memories here." In a way, Elizabeth envied his relationship with books. It was something that she hoped would be the type of familiarity she'd develop with her cake tins and biscuit trays: she believed for the day when they too would be beloved 'old friends'.

"Yes. For the most part, they hold good memories."

"How do you say goodbye? Is it so very hard?" She wondered if this was his way of saying goodbye, to more than just a collection of books. Perhaps Jensen was saying goodbye to something much more. It had not been hard to say goodbye to Farthing; she was so confused and just wanted to get out of there. It happened quickly.

He went over to a crate and picked up a volume. "Perhaps giving these books away is like saying goodbye to old friends. I like to think these are just going to a different home. I trust someone will enjoy them as much as I have. Perhaps saying goodbye to the estate will be the same." He swallowed and looked at her standing beside a crate. And Georgina. He sensed that she understood he was saying goodbye to her too.

"Elizabeth? I want to give you something: a gift to mark the start of our new home together."

"Oh?"

He walked over to the roll-top writing desk. "I would like you to have Georgina's writing desk. It is a beautiful piece, and finely crafted. I think it would make a very fine desk for a housekeeper."

Elizabeth stared at the desk. Stared at Jensen. And then fled the room in a flood of tears. Jensen gaped after her, his jaw dropped in astonishment.

She threw herself on the bed and sobbed. Just when she thought that they might be more like a regular couple, Jensen so succinctly reminded her of her housekeeper status. Through her sobs, she tried to give herself the pep-talk that had kept and held her so many times in the past year. Yes, she was his housekeeper. And yes, there were many benefits to their arrangement: she was safe; her babies had a name and a home; she was provided for. The girls aside, Susanna in particular, she was treated with respect, and yet in his eyes, in Jensen's eyes, she was still the housekeeper. The belongings of Georgina may have gradually disappeared from the house, but her ghost was still strong. He couldn't say goodbye to her after all. And then the tears started again.

Jensen came up and tapped on the door jam.

"Elizabeth?"

She refused to sit up.

"Elizabeth?"

She realised then… in the agony of hearing him say her name, patiently, mildly, that he would consider her a respectable housekeeper, friend maybe, but he would never love her as his wife. He had declared he had experienced his one true love, and he believed there was a law of life that did not allow the opportunity to love again. He had that type of love for years. Her own love survived only three short months. Oh, dear. He never would see her as anything other than someone who could dust and clean. At the start that was enough. But now she wanted more. She wanted to be important to him, more than the reason for a tidy lounge-room and a well-made bed. Fresh tears.

"Elizabeth? I am not going away until you sit up and speak to me like an adult and not some peevish child." He moved his reading chair closer to the bed and sat there quietly, waiting for her to calm. As she stilled, he spoke: a gentle flow of uncensored reflections that washed around her. "I did actually think that a writing desk would be an appropriate gift. I am not sure why it is not, but I do know that it is an item that Georgina spent a great deal of time searching for. She was particular about the pieces she collected. It is the finest mahogany. So, I assumed it would meet the taste of any discerning woman quite adequately. If it is not acceptable to you, I will sell it because I can no longer just hang onto it if it serves no other purpose than to remind me of its previous owner. So rather than just discard it in some auction house, I thought it to be a very useful piece for you. Surely that it would be more appropriate for the lady of the house to sit at a crafted desk rather than perching on the stairway or writing outside in the weather, which has been your habit."

Elizabeth turned over and sat up. Her eyes were red, and without missing a beat Jensen handed her his kerchief and kept talking. "I thought, as part of your household responsibilities, to have a place to write would be desirable since you spend a great deal of time in your notebook. And I have noticed that you have never presumed to use the writing desk. Not once. So, in my way of thinking, I determined that you would not have to think it presumptuous to use if officially it was your desk... with your own writing set and stationery and journal. I have ordered these although..."

"Jensen?"

"Yes?"

"How did you know I wrote at the table in the garden?"

"You are my wife. It is my duty to know."

"But you said I am your housekeeper."

"The responsibilities that a lady of the house holds includes managing the affairs of the house:

keeping house. We talked about this when we were engaged. You agreed this was something suitable for you to do. Managing accounts and writing correspondence are all part of those duties. And you have done so with great competence."

"Yes, I know that is what we talked about; but Jensen, sometimes I wish…"

"You are not happy?" He looked at her distraught face and swallowed. Idiot. Of course, she is not happy.

"Sometimes I wish… I was… more…"

"More? In what way 'more'?"

"More in the way of a wife…"

"Oh." He swallowed again. "Then surely the writing desk reassures you on this matter. If you think about it, Glennie never had access to that writing desk, even when she managed such duties. If you were not my wife, I would never give such a gift."

"But you said it was a gift for a housekeeper…"

He shrugged. "Yes, but only suitable as my wife, whether it is practical for a housekeeper or not."

"So, it was not intended to remind me of my place?" She sounded quite bewildered.

"Do you think that I relegate you the status of a servant? Elizabeth? Please."

"It was meant to indicate that you regard me as your wife?"

"Of course. I have never considered you staff! We are married."

"Yes... but not... married."

He rubbed his nose, with just the tiniest hint of awkwardness. "We agreed on that too."

Tears filled her eyes again. "Don't you find me the slightest bit attractive?"

He stared at her speechless.

"I'm not, am I? I am not as pretty as Georgina?"

"I don't think that is the point..."

"Then what? Am I so ugly?"

"Grief! Ugly? Where are you getting these ideas Elizabeth?"

"From you."

"How? When? I have never said such a thing! This is nonsense!"

"But it is because you have never said. You compliment what I read. You commend the type of questions I ask and the observations I make. Even what I cook, or how I keep house... but never, never what I wear or how I look. I must fail your tastes in this regard so very completely."

For a moment Jensen looked a little panicked. He took a deep breath, and gently reached out and turned her chin towards him. "Elizabeth. You are exquisite. You are lovely in every regard. But you are not yet eighteen, and that was my promise. 'That is the reason I avoid these observations... so I can..." He swallowed again. Their eyes locked in. His hand caressed the contour of her chin in a feather-light touch. "Believe me... I want to... when the time is right."

Their gaze did not shift, and so slightly she leant in closer.

There was a loud rap at the door. "Excuse me, Ma'am. Master Liam feels hot. Ma'am! He is really unsettled!"

"Coming Hilary!" She held his hand against her face without shifting her gaze, kissing his fingers. "Thank you, Jensen. Thank you for letting me know." She straightened up and hurriedly smoothed her hair. "I am coming now!"

Jensen walked into his study and stopped. "What are you doing here Elizabeth?"

"I am your wife. I came to see my husband."

"Really?"

"Yes really. Things have been so very busy with the move, and I thought I would like to spend some time with you now that things have settled down. Here in our new home."

"You are here to spend some time with me?"

"I am allowed an audience with my husband, not just at supper time, am I not?"

"Permission is not the issue. Why are you dressed like that?"

"I thought I would like to put on something... attractive. Do you like this dress? It is new. Do you think it flatters my figure? My baby-bump is almost gone." She stood up and deliberately turned around.

Jensen went to the drinks cabinet and slowly poured himself a drink. He sipped it slowly. "Elizabeth. I know what you are doing... and I want you to stop."

"But why? This is not fair! I am your wife. Why won't you treat me like your wife?"

"I do treat you like my wife... in every regard. Except one."

"But why Jensen? I love you. You know that I do. Don't you want to kiss me?"

He grimaced. And slightly shook his head and turned around to look at her. "Elizabeth this has the feel that you are trying to prove something. What exactly do you need to prove?"

"I am not trying to prove anything!"

"Nothing?" He raised his brow and gave her a quizzical grin as his eye trailed down her gown and plunging neckline. "Are you sure?"

"Perhaps I want to prove that you love me. That you are different to Bill."

"Ahh. Bill. Always Bill. What we do as husband and wife should be about us. Not Bill. Nor Georgina. It needs to be between us without the interference of the past. I don't think we are there yet. I don't think I am there yet."

"Well, I am! I don't love him. I love you. Why can't you love me too?"

"I do love you. But I will not... until you are

eighteen and am convinced that you make this decision on your own volition."

"That is ridiculous! This is my own decision! I am here, aren't I? I am a woman. I am a mother for crying out loud! I do everything else as a woman. Why not this?"

"And this... this is the petulant teenager talking. Not the woman at all. When you are eighteen, you can make that judgement. Until then, you will wait. I will wait."

"Oh, you are a stubborn man!"

"Goodnight Elizabeth. Sleep well."

"I will not sleep a wink! You know it. And the fault is all yours!" She flounced from the room and slammed the door.

Jensen closed his eyes and regulated his breathing. He took his drink and sat down at his desk, his hands shaking. He took a sip... and bowed his head with his hand on his brow. God! What if she ever changed her mind?

For a week of evenings, Elizabeth sulked in her room rather than having supper with Jensen in his study before she retired. Finally, at dinner, as the girls excused themselves Jensen raised his eyes and looked at her. "Elizabeth, it is time to come back to having supper in the study before you retire."

"Oh, I'm sorry: I am tired. The boys are demanding at the moment. I have had a very busy day."

"Are they unwell?" His brow creased in a frown.

"No... not exactly."

"Well, I am sure Marjorie can manage them for this short while."

"But..."

"Elizabeth. I require it. Please bring supper directly."

She nodded silently. She had wanted him to feel her absence. But this didn't feel like he was asking for this routine to be resumed because he missed her, but because she was being summoned to pull herself out of a mood.

He heard her walk into the study so he moved his books across so that she could place the tray. He raised his gaze to greet her and tilted his head to look her over, head to toe. She felt herself blush under his scrutiny.

"So tonight, you come dressed like a nun?" he said with a grin. She was wearing a severe dark grey pinafore and high-necked white blouse. Her hair was pulled back sternly off her face.

"I don't know what you mean Sir."

"Of course, you do. Last week you were trying to brazenly seduce me. Tonight, you look like you have taken orders. Is that really necessary?"

"Being attractive evidently displeases you."

"Are you punishing me… or yourself? I wasn't displeased, Elizabeth."

"But you never notice whether I am attractive or not."

"Do you think I don't notice you? Of course, I notice. Even in that habit I can't help but notice. I know you look older than your seventeen years… but it doesn't change the fact that you are. I want to remain a man of my word… so I will keep my promise."

"But why? I don't want you to keep that promise any more. I really don't."

"I am not convinced that is the best course as yet, so the promise still stands."

"But it is a silly rule."

"When I made that commitment, you were very relieved."

"But I thought you were old."

"I am still the same age… a little older now actually if you think about it."

"You know what I mean: I didn't know you. I didn't love you."

"And there is still more to know. That is why supper is important. It was a good idea of yours and that is why I want to continue this routine … even when the boys are unsettled, and you are tired." He lifted the plate and offered her a biscuit before he poured her tea. "And you don't have to dress like a nun. I am fine with what you normally wear to supper... even if it flatters your figure. Somehow I will suffer through noticing," he said with a smile.

There was an idea that had been swimming around in Elizabeth's head for a while. She had been watchful as to whether Jensen was true to his claim that he treated her as his wife. And he did: in private and in public. He showed her the entry made in the Family Bible, where their wedding date and the birthdate of Liam and Ben had been entered into the family tree.

But now she wondered how she could reciprocate and treat Jensen as her husband. She wasn't even sure what that would look like. What other things would a man desire from his wife... bedroom aside? She tried to recall things her mother might have done for her father, but apart from perpetual disapproval or the snide dismissal of just about everything he did, she could not recall anything that seemed to be the message of marriage, that said affectionately, 'This is my husband'. She made a study of Glennie and Joe. Here she found material that was much more to her liking. Little things. A touch as they walked past each other in the hall. A smile as they shared a private joke. A whisper of thanks as a task was completed.

When they took the boys out in the

perambulators with Hilary, she would observe couples walking in the park and try to decide what things suggested whether a couple was married or not. What she noticed was not whether they were beautiful or handsome; well dressed or poorly dressed; well-spoken or coarsely spoken. What she noticed was that there was a common notion of proximity. Proximity in standing. Proximity in talking. Proximity in walking. Proximity in sitting. Proximity in passing. The other person knew they were there. Close. Present. Even without touching. And so, Elizabeth set herself a mission to behave – less like the housekeeper and more as Jensen's wife.

The accusation of the being the petulant teenager had been a strong rebuke, more effective because the observation was given without malice. How could she behave like his wife... without being demanding? Without being intrusive. Not withholding or withdrawing... just using proximity. And this seemed more of a challenge than putting on an attractive dress and trying to mandate his attention... while he, by his own admission, fought against noticing whether she was beautiful or not, in the effort to keep what she considered was an out-dated contract.

She thought she could start with supper.

Proximity. That was her mission.

She walked into the study and put down the tray. As she put it down she stood close to his chair. She sat down opposite and drew the sitting chair a little nearer to the low table. He absently went to pour the cup, and she brushed his hand. "Please. Can I pour our tea tonight?" He looked up a little surprised but deferred to her wishes and sat back in his chair. She got up and stood by his chair as she bent over to rotate the teapot as he had a habit of doing. She turned and smiled and asked, "Am I doing this the way that you like?"

"I don't think it matters."

"No, I don't think so either... but I thought I would try it that way. Your tea is always nice."

He shrugged... a little bemused, and then nodded.

She handed him his cup and again made sure her hand brushed his. The touch was barely noticeable, but he looked at her curiously, and she sat back sipping her tea and chatted about nursery antics. Ben, chubby and strong, was developing a habit of crawling over and sitting on Liam when his brother frustrated him. She laughed and observed that she thought Liam would have learnt by now not to persistently insist on interrupting his game of wooden blocks. After a few such stories, she yawned and smiled her intention to retire. This was not new. She did so every evening. What was different was that as she got up to leave she went over and kissed Jensen on the cheek, and whispered goodnight.

She lay in bed; his side still empty, but she felt responsive to him in a way that surprised her. She thought this was just about developing his awareness of her. She wondered if he would always wait until she was sound asleep before he would come to bed because no matter how hard she tried, she could not outwait him. She focused on the clock, but the next thing she remembered was stirring to daybreak filtering through the curtains, and the sound of Jensen moving around at the washstand having his morning shave.

16.

"Jensen? Next month is my birthday. Last year I refused to remind you, but this year, I do want to prompt you and let you know what I would like for my birthday. I know what I want, and it may be something that you are reluctant to give me."

He looked up from where he was writing. "Hmm? Let me guess. If you are giving me this much notice... you would like a Ball?"

"Now that is a fascinating idea. If I wanted a Ball, would you do it? I happen to know you have a particular aversion to dancing. Would you host a party for my birthday and dance with me?" She stood there, her eyes teasing him.

"Well... would I? If you could convince me it was the thing you wanted most for your birthday, I guess I would comply. And yes, I could even give you a birthday dance. In fact – that would be my pleasure."

She collapsed into a chair and laughed. "I think I actually believe you would do this for me! You are insane! You hate dances... and yet... yes, I believe you would!"

"You know that I would."

"Well lucky for you, I do not want an extravagant gala event with shallow music or shallow gowns. I want something much more demanding."

"More gruelling than a ball with chamber music and glamorous fashion? You have piqued my interest if nothing else."

"I didn't say gruelling... I said demanding. It will demand your time and attention."

"You have my attention now. What is it that you want?"

"I want to go to the seaside."

He put down his pen on the blotter, turned and looked at her, his eyebrows raised. "The Beachside Cottage?"

"Yes. Where we had our honeymoon. I want to go there. Just the two of us... for a couple of days by ourselves before the children join us for a holiday to celebrate their first birthday. I don't know if the girls will want to come but of course, they are invited."

"The Beachside..." He swallowed... and blinked.

Elizabeth's voice was light, and she tinkled a laugh. "Well, I don't see you speechless often. Is this something you need to think about? You don't hesitate at a Ball, yet you swallow at the Beachside Cottage."

"I think you are merciless... and relentless... and I never had a hope of anything other than falling in love with you," he said half to himself.

"Oh, I think I have a tutor who is a master. He only has himself to blame if that is what he thinks."

He picked up his pen, docked it in its holder, and

rubbed his nose thoughtfully. "I think this is the woman talking…" he murmured.

"Jensen. This is very much what I want," she said quietly.

"Very well then…"

"Oh! You are wonderful!" She bounced over and gave him a hug. "There are so many things that I need to get ready! We are going to have a perfect time! I know it!"

Jensen pulled up in the buggy, and Buchanan loaded their cases. Elizabeth had taken Glennie for a few days last week to the Beachside house, to spring clean, and stock the pantry. She was confident she had prepared for this holiday with everything that was needed. Elizabeth kissed the boys one more time. "Five days… and then we will all be together. The ride with the horses will be so much fun." She tickled them and they giggled and squirmed as Hilary and Susanna held them tight.

Eunice stared with a frown and Susanna quickly handed Ben over to Glennie's arms, as she pulled her father aside. "Do we have to come? It is a ridiculously long way for a few days," Susanna complained.

"Ridiculously necessary – you are just about all grown up, so we will have a family holiday before you completely grow your wings and fly the coup. Now please help Glennie and Hilary with the boys."

Jensen held out his hand and assisted Elizabeth up into the seat. She smiled at him and waved at the boys as he flicked the reigns and drove out the driveway.

They stopped at the roadside inn. Jensen attended to the horses while she took their cases to their rooms. They met in the dining room and she indicated to the wait staff that she wanted a particular table. "I am very hungry Sir," she said with a winning smile.

Jensen said nothing but just raised his brow as he pulled out her chair for her to sit. "I am getting the distinct impression that this is something of a do-over. Elizabeth, there was nothing wrong with this trip the first time. It was perfectly appropriate given the circumstances as they were back then. You don't have to try and rewrite it."

"I was so scared and timid and mortified. I don't feel that way anymore. That is what has changed. I guess I wondered what it would be like... to do it as I am now. Although it is hard not to be distracted by thinking about what the boys will be doing. They should be eating their dinner about now."

"So very likely. Their faces will be an interesting colour-palate of vegetables and egg custard."

"Hilary will be wearing a lovely matching smear of mashed pumpkin on her pinafore and forehead."

"This sounds like we are having our normal family dinner... just miles apart," he said as he handed her a menu.

"I will make a point of not wearing my food. Besides, this is not usual. This is just us." She blushed.

"Well, that is a very pretty look, Elizabeth. What might you be thinking about?" The last time they sat here, and he asked that question, it was Bill who crowded her thoughts. This time two little boys bundled in on her attention. Would there always be someone else vying for her attention?

"My husband," she said, and she blushed again.

"Oh? What about him exactly?"

"How he is the kindest, most generous man in the world."

"That is high praise from one who is a kind and generous mother." He picked up his menu, but the items listed seemed to blur. "I used to like only the straightforward meals. It seems I have been exposed to so many dishes that I hardly know what to order."

"Perhaps order the beef." She smiled at him triumphantly. "A straightforward meal is perhaps a relief when every other part of your life remains quite complicated. That is something that has not changed."

"Elizabeth your capacity for discerning observations and sensible thinking deserves my ongoing admiration. What are you going to order?"

She looked down the menu and knitted her brow thoughtfully. "The first time I looked at this menu I was overwhelmed by the dishes. It seemed to me to be the epitome of culinary delights. But actually, it is really just a very basic menu. I was hoping for something more flavoursome… something more … special… exotic."

He almost choked and then chuckled. "I think you are going to be disappointed should you be hoping that would be your dining fare tonight. It is a traveller's inn. Perhaps we have come to the wrong place if that was your desire."

She shrugged and smiled, and then observed quietly. "We are in the perfect place and I think I will get everything I desire for my birthday." She glanced over at the door. "Do you remember Joe and Glennie coming into the room that night? They were laughing so hard. I could barely understand how they could be such good friends when they were married. Jensen, to be able to talk with my husband as a friend is a very lovely thing."

He smiled pensively. "I think friendship is a fundamental quality to hold in a marriage."

"I never even thought it was possible. But I think it is also important to be in love. One without the other means something is missing."

"I remember that last time we were here you were missing your Bill." He brought it up intentionally. Was she really over him?

Now she almost gagged. "Missing Bill? Maybe. But I don't think you realise you were casting up a very large shadow and every single thing Bill ever did was being shown up as small-minded, self-absorbed and shallow."

He looked at her intensely. "Really? You were not pining? I thought you were love-sick."

"I was pregnant sick... and my life was the most confusing mixture of ..." She paused and looked into his eyes surprised by what she saw there, and then laughed. "Oh my! You were jealous! Oh, my goodness... I never knew!"

He held her gaze for a moment. He wasn't able to deny that. He signalled to the attendant and placed their order. Then he picked up the drinks menu. "You are now eighteen. Would you like a glass of wine?"

"My birthday is tomorrow, so I am not eighteen yet and I have had wine before... at many of Mother's functions... but when I met you I was pregnant and the idea of it just made me feel sick."

"Of course,..."

"Or do you think I need to be drunk to do this?"

"No, I..."

She laughed. The anxiety was gone. She felt no fear. Rather she felt seen. "Bill had one thing going for him. He was handsome... in a very immature, schoolboy sort of way. My tastes are more mature now. That night when we sat here, I couldn't get over your eyes. Not just the colour; they seemed to see right through me... into my soul. It is the most beautiful thing... to be seen by you." Elizabeth picked up the menu again. "Remember how I told you I liked to cook? I was terrified… sharing that. I think it was a test."

"A test?"

"I think I wanted to see if you were like my family who despised my small, unglamorous aspirations. Mother was mortified that the most ambitious thing I ever wanted in my life was to work in a kitchen."

"Well, I am grateful I had the sense to hold my tongue."

"Oh no Mr Harker, you did more. You endorsed my dream even though it was messy and unappreciated by just about everyone I knew. You justified that by sharing with me your own passion for design. Jensen, I am so sorry, that your choice to be with me has crushed your dream."

"I have received much more than I lost. I hope you realise this."

"I wish there was a way…"

"Perhaps there is. I am working on a couple of ideas."

"You are! Why didn't you tell me? Will they take you back?"

"No, I don't think so. And even if they would allow it, I wouldn't want to be there now. No, the exclusion clauses of their settlement are pretty tight. But I thought about what it is in design that inspires me. Do you remember how I talked about changing and updating this dining room so that it could be more efficient and workable? They cannot stop me from consulting on jobs such as this. This would be something that would also encompass workflow and strengthening business practice... improving work conditions, and financial returns. I've never heard of anyone doing it, but surely there is a need."

She held him with her gaze, her eyes wide. "Jensen that is such a brilliant idea! You are so right. This is not architectural design, but it is a more comprehensive approach that encompasses all of those things you are so passionate about. Oh, you would be so good at that."

They ate quietly for a while. "Are you going to ask me about my other idea Elizabeth?"

"What other idea?"

"I said I was working on a couple of things."

"There is more?"

"There is... but I don't want to appear overconfident in my expectations of what you might like. I was working on this as a gift for your birthday."

"Ahh. You also sometimes fear presumption. I didn't think this was a condition that the confident Mr Harker understood. But you all gave me gifts yesterday."

"Slippers, a shawl, and a rolling pin."

She giggled. "Very clever that the boys gave me slippers that were wrapped separately but were exactly the same... just like them. I think Susanna wanted to strangle me with the shawl, and I asked Eunice if she would like to join me using the pin in the pastry classes I have arranged with Aunt Dotty. She didn't say no outright. I think this is progress."

He grinned quietly. "Yes. I think so too."

"And you gave me perfume... which I am wearing by the way." She leant over and presented her wrist, which he softly kissed. She shivered and withdrew her arm.

He noticed her blush. "Is it okay if I notice that you look particularly beautiful tonight?"

"It is always nice when you notice me."

"Hmm. I do. This other gift is something... not from the children, but from me. What you asked me that night we were here, I promised I would do what I could if I thought it was reasonable enough."

"You mean cooking? The kitchen in the house is perfect, and Aunt Dotty has agreed to show me more of her family secrets. Now I have a question for you. What is your favourite?"

"Favourite?"

"Yes, what is the favourite thing I cook for you."

"Oh... that is a hard question. There are so many excellent choices. No, actually, it is very simple. My favourite is your oatmeal biscuits."

"What? Ordinary plain oatmeal biscuits! You have patiently taste-tested all my attempts without complaint – even those things that are not at all straightforward...   always   with   a   word   of encouragement. And yet your favourite is plain oatmeal?"

He shrugged. "It was the first thing you baked for me. And you were so excited. I had forgotten what it was like to pursue a dream and delight in it. That's what I like about your oatmeal biscuits... and perhaps apple cake is another favourite. I like how you extract a critique out of me for everything you make. And besides, they both are the perfect accompaniment to a cup of tea."

"Oh, you are very odd. Eunice likes my sponge cakes. Susanna admits to liking very little, but I see her sneak chocolate fudge sometimes."

"Elizabeth. I think you are an excellent cook. You enjoy food in a way I rarely have seen. Soo... this brings me to my other idea. To celebrate your eighteenth birthday... I bought you a little café."

Her eyes flew wide open. Elizabeth choked and put down her fork. "I'm sorry... what?"

"A café. It is on Lane Street."

She reached over and took a swig from his wine glass. She started breathing rapidly. "Oh my! Oh my!"

"I confess it is a little run down... but it has all the potential for you to continue expanding your dream. Perhaps this can be my first consulting job on improving a business venture on all levels. It will be a great sampler for us to see how this works."

"A café?" Tears welled up in her eyes, and she

took another drink. Just breathe. Just breathe.

"Yes. I think it has great potential. I can't wait to show you. It has... Elizabeth? I thought this would be pleasing."

"Oh... it's..." Breathe! Elizabeth picked up a serviette and fanned her face and dabbed her eyes. Breathe...

"I am sorry; this is not what I thought. I guess my fear of presumption was more real than I allowed. We can build it up and sell it again if it is not something you want to pursue."

"Oh Mr Harker, you are a very unusual man."

"I think this time I am finding unusual quite unacceptable. My apologies Elizabeth; I had not..."

"I cannot believe that you would do this!" Her tears no longer stayed contained.

"I really misread this terribly..."

"You would believe in me so much as to buy a café? A café! For me?" Her voice shuddered and cracked. "You would invest in my dream? This has been my beautiful, impossible dream forever! Two years ago, my life was over! How is something like this even real? My own café!" Fresh tears.

"You are not annoyed?" He looked at her across the table, tears streaming down her cheeks, while she blushed under his gaze. He took his glass back and drank some of his red wine, relieved.

"Annoyed? I am the luckiest woman alive... to have met you and married you. They were going to send me to the poorhouse... like trash!"

"I also want you to have something that is independent income so you can support the boys in the event something happens to me. This would provide for you if it came to that."

"Oh Jensen. Don't talk like that. Not tonight. You are not that old. Tonight, the poorhouse is far away. You saved me from that."

"If you think I just saved you from a poorhouse Elizabeth, you do not realise what you have done for me. You have been just as generous in saving me."

"Jensen, do you really think I can do this? I will need a lot of help. Oh Jensen, please promise me we do this together. I really don't deserve this or you!"

They walked up to their rooms together after they finished their meals. Elizabeth reached the top of the stairs and gently kissed him on the cheek. "We have a long day of travel tomorrow with an early start. I have booked separate rooms tonight..." She handed him his key.

"But I thought..." He held her wrist gently searching her eyes, and she smiled disarmingly.

"This is my choice. Goodnight Mr Harker, Sir." And she slipped her hand from his grip and fled to her room, leaving him staring after her. She stood against the door for a long time, tears streaming down her face in gratitude.

17.

They left early in the morning to travel to the Beachside Cottage. It was afternoon when they pulled into the driveway. Elizabeth made her way down the hallway with a couple of boxes which she put in the dining room. Jensen carried in their bags and deposited them in the bedroom. She stood for a moment in the doorway, and then said, "I am tired from the trip. I am going to draw myself a bath and get changed so there is no need for you to rush while you sort the horses. I'll see what I can do for a light supper."

Jensen nodded. Perhaps this was something else he had misread. He thought everything pointed one way, but now it seemed like a holiday... just a plutonic aside at the Beachside Cottage. Would he rue the day he prioritised her friendship and waited for her maturity? He went out to the stable and rubbed down the horses. He did take a little extra time and a little extra care. He was always particular with grooming his horses but just now he gave them the extra attention because he thought this was more bearable than thinking of Elizabeth, upstairs, soaking away any thought of him. It was evident she had no idea how she was driving him to distraction. Her power over him now seemed entirely complete. Yet she never used it. Even that first day at the ball, as they walked around the grounds in the dark, she had thought about his reputation over preserving her life. How could a soul, instructed and groomed in social pretension; one who was used and taken-for-granted over and over; how could she be so giving? Yet this was his Elizabeth. Last night at dinner was the first time that she had ever compared him to her handsome, insolent Bill. And yet somehow, he felt he came out on top. He felt she had chosen him. Now he was not sure. Perhaps she had chosen him, not as a husband, but as a father to replace the one who had never stood up for her or the parent who never defended her. But just now... he didn't feel like a parent. Not at all.

He walked back to the house, stamping his boots on the mat near the step and he sat down and took them off, replacing them with his house shoes. He went through the hall and paused at the dining room door. Elizabeth stood near the sideboard, dressed in her wedding gown, adding some final touches to a platter of fruit, bread rolls and other savoury titbits. On the table, there was an apple cake. Finally, she lit the candelabra in the fading evening shadows and turned and saw him standing there.

She smiled, a little unsure. She wondered if he would be displeased. Would he still hold her at arm's length? Yet he had said, over and over, this was her choice. When she was eighteen. When she was sure. Well, today she was eighteen. Now she was sure. She was choosing that this incredible man would also be her husband.

She looked entirely enchanting in the candlelight. His heart swelling as there was nothing plutonic, nothing paternal, nothing but love, in what he was seeing. "You look like an angel," he said stepping forward. He smiled. "I am noticing..."

"Of all the fancy dresses that I have worn, this one makes me feel beautiful, sprinkled with care rather than beads. Mother's ball-gown was not the last pretty dress I was to wear after all." She smiled and gave him a deep curtsy.

He swallowed. "Oh, Elizabeth. Your taste is impeccable. You had so much trouble choosing this, and yet it is absolutely elegant. Perfect. You just had to learn to be aware of what you already knew." He stepped across the room.

She laughed.

How he loved to hear her laugh.

"Of course, you would say that... because I am very aware of what I think you knew all along."

"Oh?" He stepped closer.

"I think you knew from that first night we met at the Ball, that we would never just be convenience... just making do with the terrible situations that we were subjected to. I think you knew that we would fall in love... that we would be husband and wife. You knew this. I know that you did. I know that you love me as a woman. I want you to know that I am aware of it too.

He stood there, his eyes searching deep into her soul for any reservation, or hesitation. "Elizabeth?"

"Yes?"

"Would you do me the honour of having a dance with me?"

"You would dance? You don't like to dance!"

"For your birthday. Perhaps I had to find the right partner again…"

"We have no chamber music…"

He smiled and began to hum a waltz; his deep and velvety tone resonating over and around her. Elizabeth thought that it sounded sweet like rich, melted chocolate. He tilted his head and offered his hand. She smiled and curtsied. He took her hand, and humming the waltz, he spun her into his arms, and across the floor, around the chairs. It took her by surprise, and she laughed. "You have been holding out on me Mr Harker. You are a very accomplished dancer!"

"I never purported I couldn't dance. Only that I didn't like to." He slowed the music on his lips to a gentle waltz.

She looked up at him under her lashes. "Do you like this?"

"Yes. Yes, I do. Very much. Happy Birthday, Elizabeth."

Gradually the music on his lips slowed. He stood there with her in his arms. Looking down, he touched her chin and asked, "May I kiss my bride?"

Before Elizabeth could reply he kissed her... hard, passionately, and she responded with all of the painful energy of being eighteen and being in love.

They woke to the sound of waves crashing on the beach and the sun streaming through the curtains at the French doors that led to the balcony.

"Good morning Mrs Harker..." he said with a lazy smile.

"Oh! Good morning Mr Harker," she said with widening eyes. "You didn't get up to read a book this morning?" It was the first time she had woken to him lying beside her.

"I wanted to look at something more fascinating than a book this morning. How is it that you look beautiful... whatever you do; whatever time of day?"

"Huh. You have seen me after I have nursed the boys with a fever. I cannot believe that anyone can meet the expectation of perpetual beauty, when they have tended to distraught, feverish children all night.

"Ahh. And yet you do."

"Are you confessing to looking? Were you noticing your housekeeper after all, Mr Harker?" she said with a cheeky smile.

"Every moment of every day. She is so beautiful."

"Perhaps Sir, it is not the beauty of the wife, but

the eyes of the beholder that makes it seem so."

He rolled over and smothered her with kisses. "For a man my age... my eyes are perfectly sound. How exquisite you are!"

She giggled and whispered. "So, you have noticed!"

"I have."

"You do love me."

"I do."

"Perhaps it is not a once-in-a-life-time privilege after all. Perhaps it is a gift that is sometimes given whether we deserve it or not... a gift that is bigger than even a café..."

"Perhaps it is."

"Thank you for bringing me back to this little Beachside Cottage Jensen. It is here where I have learnt what it means to be loved. Twice."

The end

More Stories by Olwyn Harris

Matt's Boys of Wattle Creek

When Matthew Lawson's three sons were born, he wrote each of them a letter outlining his hopes and prayers for their futures. When he decided to give up his city job and move to the little town of Wattle Creek, he could never have imagined the effect it would have on his young family. As Matt's boys grow to maturity and find their places in their community, will his dreams and prayers come to fulfilment? Will his boys develop their own faith in the eternal God? And will they each find the kind of love that Matt holds for his beautiful Josie?

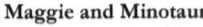

Maggie and Minotaur

"For Maggie, the mythical Minotaur represented Romance – half man, half beast. The Minotaur was a monster created from centuries of classical Greek mythology and no normal man could withstand its strength... Sooner or later she would accept that Theseus, the hero, did not exist. She knew that she would have to battle through the maze of reality and confront it herself."

Maggie Wick was shipped off to the city and high society life at the age of 12, where she would learn the way of the rich and marry into a family of influence. What could have caused her sudden return to Henderson's Gap? Can she really settle back into life on the station, with all its diversity and challenges? Will she find fulfilment in her role as a provisional schoolteacher? Will she ever figure out the "Captain", the mysterious, intimidating station manager?

When war comes to her little haven and Maggie's world come crashing down, taking her loved ones and the Captain with it, Maggie needs to find a way to survive. Will her faith be enough to protect her, and what of the Captain? Could he really be the Theseus who would do battle with her Minotaur?

Gems of Australia– 6 Part Faith Series
#1 Sapphires of Hope

"There is no way," she thought, "that I am going to use this!" She had desperately searched their cupboards for something, anything that would come close to what she needed for her catering project. She found only this old dilapidated breadbasket that looked like the sort of junk that comes from one of those tacky jumble-sale stalls..."

Andi and Jo are best friends... they do pretty much everything together. So, when Andi has a catering assignment due, and only a tacky old basket to use, Jo helps her pull off the faded decorations, revealing a time-capsule of historical information, and in order to understand what it means, Andi and Jo ask their elderly neighbour to take them to visit the farm where the basket came from. They find themselves dumped back in history at the time of Federation, embroiled in circumstances that nearly cost Andi her life and threatens the livelihood of the people living there. How can they ever hope to keep going when things are spinning out of control?

Coming Soon from Olwyn Harris

Gems of Australia– 6 Part Faith Series

#2 Rubies of Ambition

Jo and Andi travel back into another period, this time with a beautiful actress named Lillian Browning from the 1920s who suddenly returns to the town of Gum Ridge where she grew up. The prickly-pear plague is at its height and desperation has invaded the hearts of people on all levels. How can Lillian find meaning outside her shattered ambitions? Will she ever reconnect with the people in her hometown who reject her pursuit of fame just like she rejected their humble community when she left?

#3 Emeralds of Dreams

Another time-warp journey finds Jo and Andi back in colonial times and they are horrified at the living conditions of those who had no choice but to live out the term of their natural life in Australia. Dreams seem a pointless exercise that belonged to their past. When the girls meet Polly, they start to see what is below the surface. Will Polly and her young daughter Jane, ever find a new way through the hardship to invest in their future dreams with anticipation?

Children's Stories

Bush Olympics

A fun story that helps children understand that they have been uniquely created in God's sight. If the Bush Olympic coach, Mr Mopoke, can allow the animals to use their God-given talents and strengths, this wacky and wonderful team can go on to achieve great things.

Houses of Healing Series - 3 Part Series

#2 Petrea Downs

The death of her husband leaves Meg struggling to keep the farm going on her own. When she shoots and injures a cattle-duffer trying to steel her stock, she has no idea that Ben Harker is going to be the portal to the healing that she so desperately needs.

#3 The Writer's Retreat

The run-down stone cottage looked like the perfect place for Tess to retreat, not only to write her book but to escape her past. As she discovers her characters and delves into their stories, she also finds that God is delving into her own story at the same time. Her relationship with the local publican challenges her to stop running. Can she honestly confront the ugly aspects in her own story, so that God can bring them both to a place of healing?